from *Pakistan* to **Preston**

Terry Boyle (signature)

For further information visit:
www.artificialsilk.org

e-book
& additional printed copies of this book
available directly from: www.artificialsilk.org

from Pakistan
to Preston

A. T. Boyle

contributory author

Terry Boyle

ARTIFICIAL SILK

First published in Great Britain in 2012
by ARTIFICIAL SILK
www.artificialsilk.org

Text copyright © Alison Boyle
Design copyright © ARTIFICIAL SILK

Printed in Great Britain by Ashford Colour Press Ltd

ISBN: 9780957324107

dedicated to everyone who worked at
Courtaulds Red Scar and the many textile factories
now closed in the North of England
(Terry Boyle)

per C e C, sempre
(Alison Boyle)

It may have remained an evil-smelling
and explosive curiosity if not for

$$H_2SO_4 + NaOH/Cell/Xanthate = Cellulose + Na_2SO_4 + H_2O + H_2S$$

Prologue

Today there's no one except us at the edge of this world, where *chiriyaan* sing from the tops of hedgerows and mingle with wild roses and convolvulus and sloes and rhododendron. Where the sentry oaks behind it all twitched their thousand spindly wands and made something happen.

Are you watching me as I slip in by this side gate? It's invisible if you haven't been here before and don't know where to push your shaking hands through the knotweed to find the catch. I have and I do.

The factory road starts off quite smooth, tufts of daisies growing where the tarmac's bubbled and split by the sun. But bricks that used to hold up the sky begin to get in my way. That film on *North West Tonight*, a photo in the *Evening Post*, both showing a neat felling of tall chimneys down the length of Viscose Alley. It wasn't Fred Dibnah who pulled them apart.

You couldn't persuade me to come here that day could you, or any time since, to hear the moment when explosives made a brand new road of bricks, poorly laid of course, causing me to stumble today. When I think that this road might have come from Benandonner's missiles flung across the water in a giants' battle, a Causeway built in England instead, that feels easier to accept than company directors losing interest and moving the

1

business on, flitting, not facing up to the challenges.

What's left? Buried under the brick road and buried under the tarmac road and deeper down if the pipes haven't collapsed yet, the amber viscose will have set inside them anyway. One or the other, both not to be inspected again. And an underground lake, the reason the factory was built here in the first place, all seven of the bore wells are grown over by the looks of things. Some would think, so what? Not the decades of people before me, people I worked for, who worked with me, worked for me. I know that they think otherwise.

Is that you waving a little coloured flag, a message not to despair?

I know it's no flag. Or you. Whatever it is, it's drawing me off the road and I'm finding the going easier here at least.

A square of cardboard with a winding of artificial silk, that's all it is. Two materials created from wood and the man-made viscose survives. It's no surprise that the small backing card crumbles in my fingers, blows away towards Horseshoe Bend. This loose skein I'll put in my pocket, Blazing Naraanji like as not - our name for it, not the one in the Standard Shade Book. The colour will be a good match still, the sun and wind unable to fade the pigments, though they'll have tried hard enough. I don't know why I expected *everything* to be changed. That's silly. But I did.

Another colour there, signalling from under a stray brick.

It's a Putting Green green that's lasted a lot longer than its creator, Victor Hesketh - cancer a year after we closed. I'm surprised that I miss the Spectre. And you, it seems like you're following me as I head east towards the fields and trees that were drawn for us in felt-tip silhouettes. Remember those evenings when we made shadow shapes against the walls of our den? I could feel your breath, then. You stroked my hair and found the curve of my ear. You pulled me close, not so gently. The light dipped and we kissed and our eyes adjusted second by second until it was quite dark. I remember that.

Let go, Tommy.

On my visit for the Guild next week I'll tell the pupils what it was like starting at Atherton's aged sixteen, straight from school, starting at the bottom and staying to the day it was shut. I suppose it wasn't long when you think of a lifetime of working. If Mam and Dad had understood what I wanted...

Tommy, when the job's there you'd be a fool not to take it.

If I do, that'll be that.

Don't lose the chance, son.

What can I tell the pupils in fifty minutes? They'll need to find out for themselves, but what I want to say - we've always said it haven't we - how everyone should make things in their lives. Here, we re-generated cells from wood and changed them into threads for weaving. It was important. I might have stayed at school a bit longer though. Mr Southworth, Monsieur Dubois, they said I was making good progress in class, like I could be somebody. Everyone's mam and dad, I understand how they can become fixed, through no fault, their pasts shaping what they do to their children...

It's a good job, that's all we know.

We're sure on this one. Take it, Tommy.

I can tell the pupils about my teacher here - Mr P - I'll refer to him as Mr Postlethwaite of course, how we created a special

3

colour for the '72 Guild, and that's the point when I'll show them the sample windings saved at home. From coming here today I'll have the Blazing Naraanji and that green too, and I can take one of the flags. I hope the school won't find the story dull. Or me! Anyway, let's see if there's time. There won't be time for everything.

For some reason the face on that Chemistry teacher comes to mind, walking into the Lab the week the factory shut, carrying a puny cardboard box no match for his ambitions. Shy to appear greedy, he asked if he could return for more thermometers, gauges, flasks, rubber tubing, unopened filter boxes stacked as neat as the bookshelves in the Harris. We wanted him to be greedy, carry on for us when the flow of honey-coloured viscose was stopped in the pipes, when the Pakistanis, the Poles, Italians, Ukrainians, Lithuanians, Indians, West Indians, Belgians, me and you and the rest of us, when we didn't belong any more.

That school down the road though, producing three leading chemists in the North, their newfangled nylon replacing the tyre cord from here. Well, some of our machines were the exact same when the gates opened as when they locked us out, a time when new viscose factories were being built abroad with the latest machines, lower wages, cheaper prices. It's sad when you think of Simpson's gold thread works in Avenham, a family firm squeezed when times changed, the likes of Atherton's elbowing in. Not keeping up with the competition, that's what closed the both of us and hundreds of others across the North.

Redundant. It's a heavy word.

But when Tahira tells us about her new job in a new coning

department down the road in Mirpur, maybe it's just people and businesses moving on like they always did.

Maybe it's best to start at the beginning, tell the pupils I was born the week of the '52 Guild, Mam miffed to be confined, visitors annoying her with their stories about the best floats and church bands parading through the centre of town. Those pictures in the paper were all right, but not the same as being there Mam said. And Dicky N's photo of our '72 tea party table stretching the length of the street... I don't think a speck of that scene has dropped from my memory.

Children like the facts don't they, a few numbers. Well, there's over twenty-six miles of yarn on some of the cakes we wound with artificial silk, and that's Preston to Blackpool and half-way back, stopping round about Wrea Green or Kirkham. Imagine it, I'll say, how we made threads so strong from wood pulp and water and acid and other chemicals that they survive still. In my pocket. Here. And the fire - I have to fit that in. And I need to tell them about those final days, every ounce of pigment bursting from every spinning machine and them naming the last colour after me.

All the yarn's sold and gone of course, but the names, memories, maybe that's all there's left to do - gather them up before it's too late. It may already be too late. Yes, people have been asking, beyond what we've asked ourselves at reunions over the years. A local history group, a few journalists, and that TV crew coming round the house. I couldn't be bothered with any of them. Bad timing wasn't it, you so ill.

When I look back today it doesn't seem far, though I'll admit to feeling tired. Nobody's around, so it's all right, to sit. I'll sit here. No one's looking.

Over there, those specks of colour - blue, grey, black, brown in the direction of the Ribble, can you see them? They must be pigment drums toppled over. With no walls to contain them they'll have rolled in the breeze. There's a fair chance they'll reach the riverbank and sail out to sea. Who knows where from there? Maybe to Tahira in Pakistan and the new granddaughter you'll never meet. Floating colours, connections, they're beyond my reach today.

I can see right enough from here that the Power House is derelict and I feel sad for its supervisor, polishing the same surfaces for over forty years against the dirt and steam from the coal-fired Lancashire boilers. I'm sorry that his name escapes me. I'll honour him by going on a little further.

I suppose these broken tiles near the entrance might be his epitaph. I can't help thinking of spectacles crushed by a bully.

And since I'm here my feet will carry me to the edge of the site, as I knew they would.

I'm relieved to find so many small things unchanged. The same sloe hedges and wild roses, those knotted trunks of rhododendron invading like they always did, keeping our secrets for us.

Well! Of everything left standing! Part of our little den, abandoned even by the time we came to it. A huddle of oil cans, bent necks like swans, a bit of that old flooring I made from outdated factory manuals, a trapped rag that looks so familiar.

Oh Sunehri.

It's not a rag. It's your scarf, left here for too many years.

If I can catch the corner, try not to pull too hard and end up tearing it even more, maybe try tugging it along the seam where it looks a bit stronger...

By releasing your scarf this secret place begins to speak to me in metal dust and sawdust, brick dust, charcoal dust, molecules of oil and acid and petrol that fall on my tongue.

Perhaps so that I can speak of the memories that aren't yet entirely forgotten?

1

The Factory

For two hours Tommy had been be cooped up in the Lab. It was a hot day and he couldn't stand it. He started for the door. Any reason was good enough for seeing Sunehri Saleem. A smoke by the railway sidings? Going across Viscose Alley? Grabbing a Collis and following the old routes? Seeing Sunehri? Seeing her.

Tommy went back to the bench for his cigarettes and lighter, a cover if anyone asked, and slipped away while the others had their heads into cross-sections, alk-cell analysis, soda, the softness of the boiler waters and a dozen other things that needed checking.

That didn't mean no one had noticed. Victor Hesketh - he noticed everything. Tommy thought the Spectre would make a good train-spotter if he wasn't one already. The tiniest detail, sometimes from weeks, months ago, might be used for ammunition. He'd been on the receiving end often enough.

As soon as Tommy was out on the back stairwell he ran down the first eleven steps, clamped both hands on the banister at the twelfth, launched his legs to the side so that they were level with his waist, swung over the next four steps and round the corner, the cheap soles of his shoes finding temporary purchase and carrying him to the bottom. Five sprains in less than four years had found him the slickest approach.

When he stepped outside, the burst of heat dispelled some of the rage in his head. He jogged round the path that skirted the Caves and hit the edge of the factory road as the last afternoon delivery approached the gatehouse.

Instead of going across Viscose Alley, overshadowed by huge buildings on each side and wide enough for two full-size lorries to pass, Tommy went in at the end of the building he'd just left. He chose the steps that ran past the Duracol department and the Spinning department and arrived in the corridor outside the General Office. A few strides further and he'd be inside the men's canteen, making his way to the table nearest the opening to the Coning.

As the smell of cooking met his nostrils - stew? - Tommy remembered to dust his lips for crumbs, which would give away the fact that he had no reason to be here.

He casually poured some water into an aluminium beaker and caught her eye.

A few moments later she came out. No words or looks were exchanged as she made her way through. Tommy half-watched her walk towards him then past him. She took a sharp left into the women's canteen and he smiled when she stole his idea and poured herself a beaker of water.

Tommy closed his hand firmly round the little note Sunehri had just passed to him. He stood up. People looking on might think they had never met.

He liked that. A lot.

2

Distraction

On the quietest landing Tommy stopped to read the note.

May tum say piyaar karti hoon!
S xxx

He pressed the paper deep inside his trouser pocket, smoothing it down so that it wouldn't show, and lifted his face to the sunshine streaming through the window.

As he blundered to the bottom of the stairs then across Viscose Alley in the opposite direction from his work, Victor Hesketh darted into Tommy's mind and left it just as quickly. Under his feet liquid viscose was pumping as constantly as it always did from the Mixing Room to the Caves, and Tommy was running as he often did against the flow.

He was thinking about her eyes speckled with green and the curves of her body and the smooth skin at the back of her hand.

Why did they have to wait!

3

Owner of The Collis

Tommy stood at the buffers that marked the end of the branch line into the factory. Checking his watch, or rather his dad's hand-me-down, he decided he'd easily get away with another ten minutes.

A short distance beyond the buffers was a freight container with its side open. Tommy took a moment to smell the new delivery of wood pulp. Transported from Scandinavia to Preston Docks then north up to the factory siding, the scent of pine brought dreams of places beyond Blackpool and the seaside towns along the coast. It was always Ireland for the holidays, which Tommy discounted because it was family. Sunehri had been to Pakistan three times. All right, that was family too, but it was different. He felt resentful that things were always brought to him here, static, rather than him having the chance to travel to the source. Scandinavia sounded all right.

He entered the Pulp Store. It was as large as a hangar but Alfonso Giorgio was easy to spot, his Belladonna-shaded collar displaying above the neck of a standard warehouse coat. Tommy saw so much of himself in the assistant. This had been his first job at Atherton's and he'd tackled it with the attitude that if he couldn't carry on at school he'd make a name for himself at work. He'd strutted round and got noticed, done a spell at lifting trays in the Coning department, and now he was promoted and confined to a laboratory. 'Break-time Alfonsy,' Tommy called, his voice running thin in the vast space.

The handsome teenager came over, two years younger but the same height. 'Wrong,' said Fons. 'Seen that pulp delivery as you came in?'

'So? I was thinking, it's hard being the dogsbody. I've come to relieve you.'

Fons shook his head. 'I just went to the Gents.' The assistant looked round. A few operatives at the far end were sorting the bales wrapped in brown paper. Closer by, Sandra and Rosie were using what Tommy called the Little Devil's Fork to grab the standard batch of five pulp sheets and transfer it to the weighing scale.

Fons caught Tommy eyeing a Collis truck. Layered with ten sheets this way, ten sheets that, alternating up to the level of their chests, there was a 650 kilo batch of wood pulp itching to be delivered.

'What do you really want?' Fons asked him.

'Alfonsy, ever watch *Doctor Who*?' Tommy approached the fully-loaded truck.

The assistant followed like a stray. 'I used to, my friend. I'm not a bambino any more.'

'Stupid! I meant *used to*.' Tommy blushed. He still watched the programme on Saturdays when his mam and dad weren't around, but by now he'd forgotten what connection he was intending to make. 'See, I'm looking at something nice here. Not you, those stacks, neat on the stillage. What I'm saying is, take the break while you can.'

Fons scowled. 'Is it one of your tricks?'

'Just make sure that when there's no truck available you're carrying a story.' The advice sounded condescending even to Tommy's ears. He hadn't meant it that way. 'A Collis is always the best excuse though.'

Fons showed his exasperation. 'You're taking it!'

Tommy clamped two hands on the cold handle of the truck. 'Stop fretting. Like rats they are - always one within spitting distance of people if you look hard enough.'

'Rubbish!'

Fons watched Tommy set off for the goods lift at some speed. 'Back here in a quarter-hour, latest. Hear that?' he called.

It felt easy for Tommy, pressing the red button on the lift, anticipating the point where the metal cage would scrape against the side of the shaft, a rising pitch as you approached the first floor, a delayed clunk when the steel doors opened or closed. By delivering the pulp sheets he might gain a bit of extra credit from the lads to spend later.

On the Steep Floor he pushed the loaded truck to the press where Bert and Roman were standing on either side clothed in thick aviator-style goggles, rubber gloves and aprons.

'Ta,' said Roman.

Tommy nodded. 'Keeping my hand in.'

Roman coughed. 'I'll bet you are!'

'How is Louise anyway?' Tommy asked.

'Cheeky... I won't use the word.'

Tommy watched the operatives slip a sheet of wood pulp between two heavy metal plates in the press then move on down the line.

'Where's Fons?' Bert asked. 'Day off?'

'I'm helping him out a bit.' Tommy knew it would take a while for the workers to empty the stillage, and he didn't have a while. 'Anyway, I'm not going to let you two pilots hold me up. They'll be needing me.'

Bert laughed. 'I don't how the factory functioned before you arrived sucking your dummy, telling us what books to read, how to pinch your lips to say the perfect "pomme".'

'Hey, Roman,' Tommy said, 'that *Frankenstein* book I got you from the library - there's enough gore to keep even you turning the pages. I bet you haven't even tried it.' Tommy aimed for the lift. 'Fons'll pick the truck up later.'

Roman shrugged.

But Tommy still wasn't ready to return to the Lab, so he pressed the button and the metal cage scraped its way to the top floor. By now he understood how the soda dissolved the beta and gamma celluloses and how the press removed short-length chain molecules that might break when it came to spinning the viscose filaments. It gave him power, that knowledge. He rolled Sunehri's word for apple over his tongue, sensing her in that small space, *sayb*, *sayb*, enjoying the thought of the chances they could make together.

Once arrived on the third floor, Tommy stood at a distance and watched Wladyslaw and Ambrose chucking pressed sheets over the wall. He thought back to his first few weeks at the factory and the way he'd shamelessly pestered everyone he came across to tell him what they were doing and why. Very soon he'd picked up how the individual parts of the complicated

14

process of making artificial silk were connected. He'd learnt that once the wood pulp had been steeped in caustic soda it was called alk-cell, and that the alk-cell was dropped into a Pfleiderer and chewed into little pieces. The pieces were raked from the Pfleiderer into bins and sent to the Mercerising Room. After a few days the bins were taken up to the floor above the Churn Room and the alk-cell was dropped through a hole in the floor into the huge metal churns where CS_2 was added. After xanthation, the materials were dropped through another hole in the floor into a mixer, where caustic soda changed it into a viscous solution that was sent through the pipes under the road and then...

'Not you again!' Ambrose called when he noticed Tommy standing by the lifts. 'Thought you'd been promoted or summat. Or haven't you?'

Tommy registered his surroundings and ran a hand along his Brilliantined quiff. He gave Ambrose one of his looks.

'Mr P kicked you out already then?' Wladyslaw asked.

Tommy stepped back into the lift and returned to the ground floor thinking about what Mr P was teaching him about combining pigments to make new colours and how to give a customer what they wanted when it wasn't a standard shade and what to do when someone loved you and you loved them back - no, that last one was entirely Tommy's responsibility!

The doors clanged open with their usual delay. Keeping his shoulders square, Tommy walked confidently through the two Mercerising Rooms to the long, wide, corridor where the Pfleiderers ground alk-cell into one-penny size pieces. He'd always thought of them as aggressive bulldogs, heavy and ugly, that could as easily crush a kitten - or a man.

He watched one of the operatives stick a thermometer into a tall mercerising bin to check the temperature of the alk-cell, then manoeuvre the bin over a Collis and pump the truck's lever to raise the bin from the ground. Tommy was tempted to go over for a chat, but instead forced himself back to the Pulp Store, where he caught Fons's attention.

The assistant came striding over and for a split second Tommy imagined having a brother, sharing laughs, playing football or cards, nights out together.

In spite of being absent from his bench for so long, Tommy judged that leaving now would label him a coward. It wasn't an option. 'Alfonsy, your pathetic truck's ready to collect - upstairs. Now say *thank you*.'

Fons advanced with his fists up.

4

Penny Falls

'Got it in the neck, I did!'

'Not carrying a story? I told you to have a few excuses up your sleeve.' This time Tommy meant it to sound condescending. He cast a glance round the store. Hardly anyone was about.

Fons stepped closer. 'Why've you left the truck up there?'

'Tough being a dogsbody, isn't it.'

'You'd know - you're worse than!' Fons jabbed forward.

Tommy managed to dodge the punch, and smiled obviously to increase his opponent's annoyance. It felt like being in goal. This was going to be easy.

He was also aware that for anyone caught in a fight it was instant dismissal, though he'd encountered no problems when he'd got away with it.

Tommy gradually manoeuvred his opponent outside and round to the back, on to rough ground where discarded packaging was left before being taken to the tip.

First Fons ran his head into Tommy's stomach, winding him badly, then he took the opportunity to kick Tommy when he was bent double. The boots weren't hobnailed but they were industrial strength. Tommy could do nothing apart from keep his mouth shut to stop the pain and anger from flying out. They mustn't attract attention. The feeling of powerlessness was what hurt the most.

When at last he found his breath, Tommy grabbed Fons's arms and managed to pull him down. Then Fons lurched so that he was on top, pinning Tommy and spitting expletives in his face.

Above his opponent's head Tommy could see a rickety tower of empty cardboard boxes, collapsed flat. He was reminded of the Penny Falls in the arcades along the front at Blackpool. How agonising, how unbelievable it was that the pennies wouldn't cascade down the chasm to the end of the chute where his small hand was waiting to catch them.

Tommy managed to twist from under Fons's weight, aim a heavy blow at the bottom of the cardboard tower, and slither out of range moments before the materials crashed to the ground. 'Watch out!' he called. He didn't want Fons to be badly hurt, but didn't want him not to be hurt at all.

Tommy fled, looking back momentarily to assure himself that the assistant was still moving; Fons looked dazed, but alive.

As soon as he was out of range Tommy dusted himself down and sprinted across Viscose Alley. He took three deep breaths, neatened his hair, hoped there were no witnesses, hoped there were no obvious signs of the fight on his face, and walked in to the Lab. When he saw Victor peering at him from his titrations, Tommy wished he'd checked his appearance in the toilets first.

'So where've you been this time?' the colourist demanded. 'Wait for it...'

'Nowhere. Where'd you think!'

'I'll have you for your cheek.'

'Where've I been, the Spectre? Use your imagination, but you'll have to find it first.'

'I detect no smell of nicotine. It took you long enough not to have a smoke, didn't it?'

Tommy placed his lighter and cigarettes on the bench directly in Victor Hesketh's eye-line. On seeing that the box was crushed, he felt tempted to return it to his pocket. But he wasn't going to let the Spectre or anyone else bully him.

His dad's watch said an hour and three minutes before the siren, meaning at least an hour and seven minutes before he and Sunehri could be together.

Tommy picked up his work where he'd left off, then noticed Frank Postlethwaite coming his way. *Now I've really done it,* he thought.

'Mayor likes that last shade.'

'What? I mean, pardon, Mr Postlethwaite?'

'John Stubbs.'

'On the Guild Committee?'

'He phoned ten minutes ago when you...'

Tommy cut in to block any questions about where he'd been. 'Mr Postlethwaite?'

'Yes?'

'I'm pleased about the Mayor, but see, our shade...'

The Duracol manager smiled. 'Yes lad?'

'I think I can make it better.'

'How better?'

'Dunno.'

'You want to carry on for a bit longer?'

'If I can.'

Frank thought about it. 'Till teatime tomorrow any good?'

Shukriya, Tommy thought.

'That will leave us with a week to finish up.'

'Thanks Mr P!'

The manager strode away to answer his phone while Tommy removed a batch of dried yarn samples from the filter papers. He washed some new sample shades on the small four-armed spindle, put them in the oven, slotted another spindle into the triangular frame, wound off some yarn for a reference card and travelled the familiar routes from where he was sitting now to the rows of coning machines where Sunehri would be standing, working, thinking about being with him.

All of his thoughts, always, lead to her - and he hoped it was working both ways.

5

The Coning

Moving along the half-stairs, short-cut to the Spinning, past the Jet Room where the women always try to catch my attention, through the Cakewash and the Cake Sorting and Packing, a left at the end through that opening in the wall.

Row Two, a sign above her head, 75/18 the denier for today.

There she is standing, working, watching yarn wind off hundreds of cakes a foot from the floor, stationary and bottom-down, yarn constantly winding from the cakes below to the cones above, from the cakes below to the cones above, from the cakes to the revolving cones above.

Full cones packed and despatched to weaving mills in unfamiliar places, receiving yarn for making up beams for the cloth's warp, for weaving fine dresses, dress linings, surgical products, curtains, upholstery, knickers. Woven viscose flowing in flags and banners. Other coning workers in other factories winding yarn from cones to bobbins, cones to bobbins, or cones to pirns for the shuttles. Not here, not you.

A broken thread? The winding stops. Your fingers move fast and maybe you can't even describe each move in the making of that weaver's knot, if I asked you. You restart the winding, eyes moving quickly, on the look-out for flaws, eyebrows pinched, concentrating. Your treacle-black plait draws a line down an ironed blouse tucked neatly in to a plain cotton skirt that falls just below your knees. Brown tights, boring colour, lighter than your skin.

The machine stops again. A poor winding? You strip off loose yarn to reach the properly wound part of the cone, knot the new ends, restart the machine and put the stripped yarn in that little cotton pouch tied round your waist - not too much wastage or your wages will be docked. They won't be docked. It doesn't work like that any more. The managers are too soft or the workers too clever. The smokers keep cigarettes and matches in theirs, next to a bit of stripped yarn. You collect most of yours, *for honesty* you call it.

The machine's stopped again. The winding is finished. You pick up a cone, stick a label inside the core - shade name, run number, yarn denier, a tracking system unchanged since the factory began. You put it on a tray on the sloping shelf above, slot it on a peg.

Oskar, one hand gripping each handle, raising a full tray too high - it's heavy, not that heavy - taking his time, taking too long. I've done it myself, enjoyed everyone's eyes on me, before you came.

Sunehri, you're the only one not looking at him. All right, I'm making this seem exactly how I want it to be...

Parvin and Michelle and Maryana, they can't take their eyes off him. Moving like a dancer, Oskar places the tray on a three-shelved trolley in the alley at the end of the machines, ready to be sent down the runways to the inspection table, newly-built runways set like spokes on a wheel, converging on the table in the middle. A metal track of rollers where the trays run down, trays with six pegs and six cones, a peg through each core, one denier on the track at any one time.

Parvin chooses a cone, inspects it for damage. Broken filaments? Single filaments of small loops? A few blocked jet holes that have reduced the denier? I can't see her as clearly as I can see you.

She's found something. Is it slubs or wound-in waste? Too many knots laid diagonally across the surface and that cone will be downgraded, sold at a discount or not at all.

If I'm lucky my love, *mayri jaan*, Mr P will tell me to come directly to the Coning to collect a trial spinning cone, for keeping in the Lab with the standard cones, for future reference.

Aren't I already there? Standing close to you?

I don't know. *Mujhay naheen patta.* It's getting harder to tell the difference between what I see because my feet have taken me there, and what I gather from the places where my mind takes me.

6

Burning for Love

The siren went at 5.30pm. Tommy had already looked at his watch a dozen times in the past minute. Although he was uneasy admitting it, part of him wanted to stay in the Lab and put extra time into the new shade. Then again, he'd wasted almost an hour on the other side of the Alley today. Seeing Sunehri was never wasting time, but there was no way he should have had that fight. He thought of his dad.

Tommy said goodbye to Jean and Melville, the only ones in, and raced downstairs. Outside, he lit a cigarette and headed south-east towards the river at the edge of the site. He walked quickly in the evening sunshine, but in a way that wouldn't catch anyone's attention.

When Tommy reached the sloe hedges he took a right, then a left, and pushed through the overgrown rhododendron. He tapped the end of his cigarette against a twisted trunk, put the stub behind his ear, and kicked the door open.

He heard an intake of breath. She was already here. He hadn't meant to scare her.

He stepped inside and Sunehri came to him, their mouths finding each other, the door closing behind them with the force of their two bodies. He felt elated, angry, happy, jittery. He

24

didn't know what he felt. Tommy stretched his hand behind his back and shoved the bolt across.

After a while they found a place to sit in the clutter. They sat awkwardly, in silence.

'See what you think of this one,' Tommy blurted out, giving her his cigarette lighter. He formed a shape with both of his hands and raised it to make a shadow against the wooden wall.

When Sunehri flicked the lighter switch he saw her green-black eyes following the animal's shadow as it bounded over a raised knot - which on the scale of the landscape of his fingers was a cut tree stump in a forest. And on the edge of this movement Tommy knew she would speak; it was the way she shifted, gathered herself up.

'Your eyes are the colour of Mirpur Lake at this time of year,' she said softly. '*May Khargosh say mohabbat karti hoon.*'

'*Khargosh?*' Tommy asked.

Sunehri nodded. 'I love you, Rabbit.'

'Correct,' he said. 'It was a rabbit.'

Sunehri rolled the lighter wheel to broaden the flame, then she let it die. 'I wish my abaa was here.'

'Your dad, in here?' Tommy snorted. 'With us?'

'I mean this country, in Preston, at home with me and Maa.'

Tommy touched the back of her hand. She turned it over and he took the lighter. It felt smooth and warm, changed by her.

'We played this all the time when I was a *choti.*' Distracted, Sunehri lifted the lid of a box by her side and chose what appeared to be the best candle. She was disappointed to find that it was two broken limbs held by a central taper, so she put it back. Her hands were now free to form a new shadow shape.

25

Tommy flicked the lighter open so that Sunehri's shape would be cast on the wall, but then he watched his own hands swallowing hers, and they fell together on the uneven floor.

Sunehri sat up. '*Ooooh*! Tommy, you have burnt my finger!' The flame was extinguished but in the half-light he could tell that she was cradling her left hand. 'It hurts, Tommy.'

'Sorry, I'm really sorry.'

'You say *Maaf kurna* to mean sorry.'

'I mean it!' Tommy said. He could feel her breath.

Warmed by the afternoon sun, the space felt more stuffy than Saturday morning at the baths. He would never see her there.

She stroked his hair, found the curve of his ear.

He didn't move.

Sunehri grabbed the back of Tommy's head, pulled him close, not so gently. As the light dipped further they kissed and their eyes adjusted second by second.

She shifted, and the cold candle glanced her pulsing skin. She desired its illumination but not its heat. 'Use this instead - you do it, Tommy. Melt the wax to join it. Stick it to a base.'

For a few moments Tommy did nothing, then he began rummaging round the den. He found a rough square of metal that from its weight felt like an off-cut of steel. He fixed the candle and lit it, saying, 'Let me see your finger.'

'It is burning quite enough, *shukriya*! Do not bring that candle any closer.'

Tommy hated it that one minute he felt like he knew everything about her, the next she was like a bear with a thorn.

Was she afraid of him?

Certainly, he was petrified of her ability to hurt him.

They listened closely. The rhododendron bushes slapped their waxy leaves against the roof and their ears picked up the sound of the grand oaks stirring along the riverbank.

Tommy circled the candle and its light fell on the many different kinds of *broken*: short lengths of brass rod and lead pipes, rusty nuts and bolts with nothing to join themselves to, a large motor, thin squiggles of wire, a cluster of canisters with dark oil congealed down the lines of their swan necks, a pile of old factory manuals.

'What are you smiling at Tommy?'

'Nothing.' He pulled at a bundle of documents and read out their titles: '*Duracol Manager's Handbook 1968, Keep the Collis Truck Rolling, A Potted History of Atherton's Viscose 1960.*' He held up a maintenance manual for a Coning machine. 'Look Sunehri, bedtime reading.'

She ignored him and chose a book with a water-damaged cover. '*Cleaning the Pfl...* I cannot say this.' She let the book fall from her hands.

Tommy caught it.

'Pfleiderer,' he said, and looked inside. 'Filling the Topham Box, Matching Yarn Samples, Spinning.'

Sunehri scowled. She held him round the wrist. '*Maray jaan*, you are perfectly ready to learn about clothes - *kapray*.'

'Sounds boring. Look, and there's a book called *Pfleiderer Facts* here! Go on Sunehri, try saying it.'

'*Kapray*, clothes,' she said. 'And we will start with this kind of clothing. It is very easy to remember - *kameez*. You know the word for shirt. So, say: *Yay kameez mayri hay.* This is my shirt.' Sunehri began to unbutton Tommy's shirt from the neck.

She placed her hand on his bare chest. 'And this. Say it, Tommy: *Yay chaathi mayri hay.*'

'Err, you mean this?' Tommy asked, pointing at his chest.

She nodded.

'*Yay chaathi... mayri hay?*'

'Good.' She pulled his shirt open fully and leant in to kiss his body. The candle illuminated his skin. 'What are these, Tommy? There is a big scratch, and these bumps here. Your skin is blue. What is this? Bruises?'

'Nothing.'

'You are lying to me.'

7

Longest Shadows

Sunehri looked directly at Tommy in a way that he couldn't escape, though he'd have liked to - a lot. With his mam and dad, Spectre Hesketh and the others, it was always possible to wriggle out.

'What have you done, Tommy? Your knuckles too. Was this today? Has this just happened?'

'*Naheen*,' he said. 'Come on, Sunehri...'

She didn't respond.

Tommy stroked her arm. 'Look, I banged into something in the Cake Wrapping, that's all. Stop fussing.'

'What were you doing there? You work in a laboratory now.'

'Oh come on Sunehri, keep going with what you were doing before you started to rile me.' Tommy dived forward and tickled her under her ribs, at the side where he knew she would be unable to resist.

Sunehri laughed, then shuffled forwards and undid the final button of Tommy's shirt. He helped her remove it. 'Now we will do the stomach.' She sounded more severe than before. '*Yay mayra payt hay*. Say it.'

'*Yay mayra*,' Tommy croaked, and before he could finish, Sunehri's hand moved swiftly down to his thigh then to the inside of his thigh and down to his feet, '*Paaoon*,' she instructed. 'Feet. Say it.'

'*Pa*... it's like *piyaar*.'

'Not really,' she said, kissing him to stop the words, even ones about kissing and love.

They smelt the wax and the dust and he felt her breasts and kissed her shoulder and her neck and lips. He knew those lips.

Since last September he'd spent his days like a blinkered animal, trying to keep the thought down that the world was against them and there was no way it would work out. '*May tum say piyaar karta hoon*,' Tommy murmured. 'I love you,' and he remembered all the many reasons why they shouldn't be together. Mixed relationships weren't exactly the route to winning friends and influence, were they! Victor Hesketh, Idzi, maybe Sunehri's family for all he knew, Mr Cuff at the corner shop for definite - he needed their business but always went quiet when certain customers came in. Grandma Betty liked everyone. His mam and dad, they wouldn't be pleased to hear the words *I love Sunehri Saleem* spouting from his mouth. It felt like a silent army was against them. How could they fight it?

The deep, insistent rhythm of a diesel engine filled the space and Tommy broke away from her. It was unusual for vehicles to come down this end of the site. He realised he was shaking.

Sunehri shifted, and knocked over a container.

Tommy shushed her. Vapour filled the space. He felt like he was choking. They had stayed too long.

She blew on the candle then stood up. 'I don't want it to run onto me. It is dangerous Tommy. It might set fire.'

He began to fasten up his shirt.

'*Main nay jana hay*,' she said. 'I have to go - the last bus. Maa will be worried.'

I want to be with you, Tommy thought. He said, 'Tomorrow night, there's a show rehearsal. I've got a rehearsal.'

'I am busy too, looking after my cousins Umair and Yasir. We will send a note.'

'Who will send a note?' he asked.

'We can decide tomorrow.'

Tommy grabbed her arms. 'Me or you?'

'Everything doesn't have to be decided now.'

Their den was cracked by a thin light. They were aware that outside the sun would almost have disappeared.

He stroked her face. 'Going to the bus stop, then?'

She smoothed her clothes then un-plaited and re-plaited her hair in a way that looked easy and he thought probably wasn't. 'I have to go right now, Tommy!'

'I get the point.'

Sunehri reached the bolt first and yanked on it. It stuck as usual, so she shimmied it to release the last quarter-inch. A fresh shower of rust joined the little pile building up on the floor. She wanted him to finish dressing quickly. She didn't turn round.

In his mind Tommy saw their two shadows stretching far across the fields. 'My bicycle,' he said, 'we can go that way.' *Nicolas will see us*, he was thinking, *or worse, Embley*.

He didn't know what to do.

Mujhay naheen patta.

What if they went through the barrier together? They had not risked that before. He was frightened of risking it.

31

8

The Gatehouse

They made their way through the undergrowth, Sunehri walking in front on the narrow path, their eyes cast down against a low sun. In the far distance the two massive cooling towers threw their cloaks over the factory and Tommy saw the crazed twigs of the oaks spiking the orange sky.

He found the scene beautiful, but he was filled with questions. The world had changed since they'd gone to their secret place tonight, and he wasn't completely sure he liked it. Not all of it, anyway.

As he dragged the front wheel of his bicycle out of the rack Sunehri began walking away from him. 'I will go now. I will walk ahead.'

Tommy watched her go. There was no other movement, nothing except the sound of her running away from him. 'I hope your hand,' he called, 'it'll be OK. You might get a blister, I suppose.' He paused in the awning of a building and tracked her progress at a distance to make sure she was all right.

Sunehri went beyond the barrier at the gatehouse and Tommy was about to move when he heard voices.

Two men he didn't recognise passed close by.

He slunk back, wondering if they were inspectors at the

Water Softening plant. More likely trespassers at this time of night. As a boy his dad had shown him a pond between the den and Horseshoe Bend. It was in the middle of fields that you would only investigate if you had good reason. Marked by a sign sunk into the mud, NO FISHING, it always gave up a catch and the fish were miles better than at the chippie in town.

These men weren't carrying rods, though. Tommy decided they must be prospecting for a future raid. Or they were inspectors at the Plant, unlikely to be carrying fishing rods!

Once the men had gone out of sight Tommy set off, staying alert for other surprises.

He left the heavy shadows of Viscose Alley as a double-decker passed in the direction of Preston. He saw that the bus shelter was empty, yet he couldn't see Sunehri on the bus. She must have chosen to sit on the other side. It looked like only a few of the seats were taken, so why had she not stayed in view, sat on this side if she didn't want to attract attention by waving to him?

The lights of oncoming traffic pricked Tommy's eyes as he arrived at the barrier. He ran his hand through his hair and was surprised to find the part-smoked cigarette still in place above his ear. He was tempted to light it but resisted. He leant on his handlebars, doubting he had enough energy to cycle home.

The gatehouse had a glass hatch on each side that the commissionaire opened when goods drivers were handing over their papers. Nicolas slid the hatch part-way across. 'Walking all the way, Tom? Might as well bed down for the night.'

Tommy nodded sullenly.

'Where you been then? Working late?'

'That new Guild shade.'

'Right you are. Mek sure you stick at it.' Nicolas chucked his head. 'Seen you, I did.'

Tommy looked up properly at the junior commissionaire's face, which was lit from behind by a lamp. The gatehouse always appeared cosy to Tommy, with its plumped-up cushions and the glorified office chair. But if you looked closely you could see where a few bits of foam were missing from the armrests - a testimony to night shifts with nothing apart from the Open University on TV. Tonight there was an empty packet of crisps next to the deliveries register, a can of pop, and Mr Embley's fountain pen with the lid off. He'd heard Nicolas being reprimanded about that fountain pen more than a few times, as well as for not keeping the place tidy - the boss might pass with no advance warning.

At this moment Tommy remembered that he sometimes found Nicolas's grin annoying, threatening even, though he knew he was being ridiculous. They must be about the same age. He lit the cigarette and looked away. He saw that the land had drawn a line under the sun, and he felt the darkness of being without her. A faint glow above the light-line hinted at the possibilities, but... he sucked in and was comforted a little by the startling *naraanji* of the cigarette's tip.

Nicolas opened the window fully. 'Seen you round the Pulp Store. Earlier.'

Desperate not to lose the single place they could be alone together, Tommy was relieved that Nicolas hadn't spotted them near the den.

'Embley's on tomorrow morning. So, I won't be seeing you!'

Tommy gave the commissionaire one of his looks. The window was closed. He swung a foot over the puckered bicycle seat and positioned the pedal using the front of his shoe. The sun fell the instant he took his eyes off it, and he spat the stub of the cigarette into the gutter, thinking... *I love you. I'm certain of nothing else. So why do I feel alone?*

He might catch a glimpse of her at breakfast or dinner or in between. If not, they could meet in those quiet toilets on the ground floor. Or if not, there might be a trial spinning cone he could persuade Spectre Hesketh or Mr P he'd collect, to save their legs. Or if not, it would have to be the day after, which meant thirty-four hours apart minimum.

Every crank of the chain ratcheted up another hour away from her. Tommy felt like he was going mad, but in a not completely unhappy way.

9

Laal / Red

I sit in front of the mirror. Both my eyes are bloodshot. On this occasion having bloodshot eyes makes everything look like it's shot with blood. And there's a red mark on my right cheek. How did that get there?

I need a deep red pigment to make the new shade sing. So where is it? On my cheek? Scrape it off while singing a song?

Don't be stupid, Tommy!

Next thing I know I'm putting on my football socks. As I grab the rib, I notice the undersides of my nails - stained red, and for some reason not a surprise.

What I am surprised about is the colour of my football socks. I play in the Factory Blues team and our strip is a blue shirt, black shorts, white socks. These socks I'm putting on are unmistakably red.

Is that the red you need Tommy? The red for that shade?

I'm wearing the colours of our enemies in the league - Ribble Motors. Does that mean I have to be their goalie now? What happens if I find the pigment I'm looking for? I don't have to play for the opposition? I don't want to play for Ribble Motors!

I'm sweating and I'm not even on the pitch. I'm not even moving. I'm in my bedroom staring at a triptych of reflections.

One, two, and three.

On the left flank Jacko appears. He starts screaming at my mirror image, demanding to know what I'm playing at. He's telling me I have to change my kit now, now, now, NOW!

Is that me or my mirror image you're referring to?

Pheeeeeeeeeee!

The ref appears in mirror number three on the right and he starts screaming his whistle down my ear, telling me to get going, get started, don't do nothing! It sounds like an Al Jolson song. MOVE!

By looking in the centre mirror I can see that their striker's breaking in from the left. *Their* striker means *my* striker, the one I used to have, and he's coming straight for me. Is there time for things to change back? Return to normal? Because this is way out from normal. The striker is Jacko and it's me against him for the final score. That's about the worst it can get.

And the ref's still shrieking his whistle.

When will you stop blowing that thing?

I'm trapped in the wrong colours, that's what it is.

The sound of frustration booms in my head. Someone went shopping for me. They came back with nothing near the description I gave them, left the list behind. They've gone and bought red socks instead of white, that's what's happened. It isn't my fault the fans - all eight of them - they've started jeering at me from the line. It's not my fault I'm a traitor.

Leave me alone!

I look up. The white clouds high above the pitch have turned red. Will they rain blood?

I look down. A deep stain seeps from the place where my

boots touch the pitch, *laal* flowing from the stripes in my socks, bleeding away the red to prove I want no part of it. I promise.

Blimey, Jacko's coming nearer and nearer, and his boots are about to crush that daisy growing in the grass less than a yard away, flat silky petals that used to be white now beating, beating like molten iron. The whistle stops and I'm at the kitchen sink, my ears pulsing. *It was that bloody ref's whistle.*

We've eaten pie and chips for tea, and I'm wondering why the tomato ketchup left on the plates is the only thing that isn't red. Because it was the only thing not red before?

What's happening to me? I was in my room. I was on the football pitch. I'm not on the pitch any more.

I run up to my bedroom, avoiding the two creaky steps - I always do that. I sink on the padded seat in front of the dressing table and the air sighs through the cracks.

At last, something familiar.

In the centre mirror I can see that the mark on my cheek has turned white, an opaque white that sits strangely on the pinkness of my usual skin. Then I remember that rare cloudy marble, the one I had in my set as a young lad and lost and never could get another of though I searched in every shop and begged for swaps and asked strangers to look out for *the one*. It never came.

And now my eyes are completely white. I feel the sadness of losing that marble all over again. Then I realise something. I have two marbles for eyes, two white eyes. It's like I've got my old marble back and gained an extra one.

So who's complaining?

10

Layers

Before his parents began to stir Tommy was getting dressed, and it was taking him ages. He'd found pieces of sawdust and metal stuck in the fabric of his trousers and he'd had to dust them down. They were his only work pair.

He tried getting away with wearing the previous day's shirt but noticed an oil stain on the sleeve, so he balled it up and chucked it at the bottom of the wardrobe. He'd hand-wash it when his parents weren't around. An oil stain wasn't a surprise, but the way he'd got it was part of something bigger that must be kept from them, for now. He grabbed his last fresh shirt from the hanger, the word *kameez* silently running across his tongue, and *Yay kameez mayri hay*.

Tommy slipped his torch into his pocket, thinking it might be safer than using a candle, or a lighter come to that. *Yay mayra payt hay*. On cue, his stomach rumbled. Once out on the landing he pulled his bedroom door to, leaving enough of a gap for his arm to manoeuvre the stack of books into intruder position.

He went down quietly, avoiding the two creakiest steps, and lifted and dropped the latch at the bottom so successfully that he was convinced he deserved a commendation. If only someone else had witnessed it. *Stop it, Tommy*! He suppressed a laugh.

In the kitchen he made his usual doorstep of toast, and slapped the treacle on so thickly that it ran over the crusts like sooty lava, making it difficult to do anything else at the same time. *Not ideal when you're in a hurry.* He washed the toast down with a few swigs of tea and went to the sink to brush his teeth. Black saliva exploded like gunpowder on the white enamel. He swooshed some water round, wiped his face on a pot towel, and on his way out grabbed the packet of grease-proofed sandwiches from the table. It was convenient to assume they were for him. When Tommy slammed the door he cursed himself for wasting the care he'd taken up to that point.

It was a bright morning as he cycled off with the torch thumping against his thigh. He'd forgotten his carry-bag. The torch would survive, while the sandwiches in his other pocket might not be recognisable by dinnertime.

Tommy couldn't often afford to eat in the canteen, though there was always plenty of water going for free. By sitting at the end table in the canteen drinking water while looking in at the entrance to the Coning department, he was merely demonstrating how much he valued it, wasn't he!

Tommy slowed to a crawl at the end of Sunehri's road and wondered whether she was eating her breakfast or getting dressed or brushing her hair or teeth. He wondered what her kitchen table was like, her bedroom, her bed, her eiderdown. Maybe she used blankets woven by her family. He'd like to see them - the patterns, colours, *rang*. He'd like to see her. Now.

He accelerated dangerously through every junction and passed Mr Embley in the gatehouse fifty-five minutes early. The commissionaire was too busy saluting the technical manager to notice a junior employee, and Tommy resented him for it.

Tommy parked his bike and took a route through Atherton's that his present job gave him no reason to take, and he put his shoe against the door of a wooden storeroom there was no reason to use.

Inside, the scent of her, burnt wax, musty paper, petrol, mingling with the Atherton familiar background stink. He stood his torch out of the way then lined up a brood of dented containers along one wall. When that was done he tugged at a clump of tarpaulin and was rewarded with more grime landing all over him. He could taste it on his tongue too. Tommy was about to use his sleeve to wipe himself when he remembered there were no clean shirts at home, and he had nothing to change into here. So he closed his eyes and ran the back of his hand across his face.

When Tommy opened his eyes he was startled by what he saw. Rows and rows of workers were crammed into the den. They stood orderly and neat in their overalls, alert like soldiers on guard, ready to take commands. His skin prickled at the sense that they were not under his control but someone else's, someone out of sight who might order the firing of the rifles at their sides. It was an army, and it was looking straight at him.

At him, or through him?

Maybe he was surrounded!

Tommy span round and felt foolish to see the familiar mess, the background of broken panels held together by a few grasping old rivets.

He dared not turn again, not straight away. But the army might be assembling their guns. It might already be too late.

Unable to resist, Tommy swivelled and saw that the brigade of workers had gone. *Where to?* Slunk into the cellulose in the wooden walls and floor, ready to be extruded and re-generated in the right conditions to make filaments of artificial silk as strong as time? Maybe he and Sunehri were altering the decades of memories brought here, made here, left here for others to care for. If they were just layering their own memories on top of a solid foundation, wasn't that all right, sufficiently respectful?

Tommy dropped to his haunches and began sorting the out-of-date factory manuals that were strewn across the floor. He made batches of a more or less even size and state of preservation - there wasn't time to judge the value of their contents - then kicked the rejects out of the way and sorted again. Where one volume was slimmer he paired it with another to make up the target height. He checked the time. Ten minutes to go.

He stood up to judge the effect. Initially he was pleased with the smooth appearance, which reminded him of Noel's newly-laid lino, but the printed titles soon began to shout their orders...

> *Flushing the Jets - Health And Safety Manual 1949 - Lessons from Hooke's Micrographia* (RIPPED COVER) - *Coning Machine 58723-757 - Chemical Hazards 1963 - Pfleiderer Facts - Topham and Stearn* (UPSIDE-DOWN - LEAVE IT) - *Toxicological Impacts - Bevan and Viscose - USA Manufacturing - A Potted History of Atherton's Viscose 1960 - Good Darkroom Practice* (HE WAS WORKING ON IT)

Tommy realised that a few reject ends of woven viscose would have covered the words and made it more comfortable to sit on, or even better, lie on. Still, being here together no matter what it looked like was an improvement on pretending to read a book in the Reference section of the Harris, a SILENCE sign reprimanding each glance away from her face.

When he went outside Tommy felt dazed by the sunshine. He picked his way carefully along the weeded paths and slipped into the factory through one of the many side entrances.

The Duracol Manager emerged from his office as soon as Tommy came in.

I've got a secret, was Tommy's first thought. He said, 'Morning, Mr Postlethwaite.'

'Good to find you keen, lad.'

'As we haven't much time, I've come in a bit earlier.'

Mr Postlethwaite smiled and Tommy set his things out on the bench. It occurred to him that it was strange Sunehri had given him the word for kissing, *choomna,* long before she had kissed him. Months before.

Sunehri Saleem, always one step ahead.

Where would she take him next?

11

Giant's Causeway

Tommy worked hard all morning and only lost concentration when his stomach told him to eat. At this rate there would be no chance to meet her. The latest card winding in the reference drawer wasn't far off a match to the example colour provided by the Guild Committee. It wasn't near enough to satisfy him either, and they were running out of time.

He unwrapped the misshapen greaseproofed sandwiches on his way out of the Lab, noting the ham and pickle contents with his mam's stamp on them: two evenly-cut slices with a slapdash filling. His dad's sandwiches were entirely different: smooth and even on the inside and rubbish at showing off.

Part-way to the Caves he found he couldn't go any further. It was a silly idea, but he sensed that Sunehri was compelling him to change direction.

So he went through the centre of the Spinning department and past the middle block made up of the office, Jet Room and toilets. His new note to her, written in the middle of the night, was stuffed inside his pocket.

As he approached the opening to the Cakewash he stopped. A shape had caught his eye. He reversed two paces and saw that someone was standing at the far end of the corridor.

A simple blouse as *neela* as a summer sky, a long black plait making a vertical line to the corridor's dark-tiled horizontal.

He went to her and they found each other's lips, clung to each other.

Tommy soon pulled apart, whispering, 'I have to go. I need to get down to the Duracol. *Maaf kurna.*'

Sunehri smiled. 'Excellent pronunciation and I do forgive you.' She neatened her hair and tucked her blouse in to the home-made waistband. 'I must go too.'

He caught her hand and passed the note into it. 'Bye.'

'*Salaam*,' she whispered, waiting for him to leave.

Sunehri unfolded Tommy's note in the gap between his departure and hers. She liked the neat script, learnt from his mam, who didn't do much writing these days apparently - the only two people abroad being her sisters in Ireland.

> *Our place tomorrow, 5.35 at the latest.*
> *Don't be late. Get there on time.*
> *I'll be waiting for you, waghaira...*
>
> *Tommy*

Tommy retraced his route to the Caves and kept up a fast enough pace so that no one would stop him for a chat or a challenge. He grabbed the banister with both hands at the turn to save a few seconds. At this rate he was in danger of reaching his destination before he'd stopped trembling.

He eventually slowed along the snaking corridor and dipped in to the Gents. In the mirror he noticed dirt nestling in the corners of his mouth, and there were breadcrumbs decorating his shirt. Why hadn't she said anything? Didn't she care about kissing him when he looked like this?

Tommy washed his hands and ran the wetness through his sculpted hair, stoking up what his dad called a Blackpool Beach wave, then took a few long breaths to quieten his hiccups.

He sauntered in to the Caves, nodding at Harry and Naseem in the office as he made for the pigment drums. He'd always liked it here, where the pigments were weighed and blended then transported to the Spinning department and pumped into the hoppers on top of the machines.

At the far end of the building the enormous tanks stored the liquid viscose that had come through the ducts under the road from the Mixing Room. Once fully aged, the liquid went through filtering and on to the next stage of manufacturing Atherton's artificial silk.

Most of the pigment drums were waist-height and Tommy found it easy to weave between them. He stopped to swivel a container here and there and read its label. At any time he had access to every shade on the books and the thread samples wound on to the two-by-four backing cards stored in Mr P's room, but Tommy already knew there wasn't a winding for the intense *laal* that filled his mind. It was the perfect red to make the perfect gold, and maybe it didn't even exist.

Tommy prised the lids off a few dull shades. Nothing.

Behind a cluster of larger drums he spotted a 25 kilogrammer, its label peeling and grubby. He could just make out a short colour name followed by a series of numbers. He scrambled closer to find that the seal was intact. The label said "Red". This had to be it! If he was right, he'd ask them to collect a sample so that a new test spinning could be completed before the end of the day.

Tommy stepped up on to the nearest drum and hopped across the top of several more, their uneven surfaces reminding him of the Giant's Causeway as a child.

He was almost there when one foot skated across a lid, and although as a goalie he was used to having control of his limbs, his other foot flipped the lid off the drum he wanted. The lid skimmed through the air and crashed into a measuring can. Tommy cringed as the two objects danced on the tiled floor. He didn't turn towards the approaching footsteps.

Looking down, he realised that he was standing with one leg inside a drum of brilliant red liquid pigment, and that his right shoe, right leg, right sock, left shoe, his trousers, shirt, hands - everything was stained red. At least he was close enough to see the label properly now: "Red 1175-62".

Tommy registered that Harry and Naseem were walking towards him. Idzi was one step behind. He felt thankful that the audience didn't include Alfonso Giorgio. He recalled a holiday as a boy, the crackling fire they'd made from driftwood carried all the way from the Causeway to their boarding house. There

47

was a fearful story on his dad's knee about the Irish giant Finn mac Cumhaill and the Scottish giant Benandonner and a terrible need for the crossing of the water. He remembered the goodnight kiss from his mam that made the world feel safe. Embarrassing but true.

As it spread across the tiles, the red pigment looked like blood seeping from his feet. He tried to find comfort in the idea of their den but instead the words on his newly-laid floor mocked his mistake...

Potted History Combustibles Carbon Disulphide (**WHAT**) *Good Darkroom Practice (**A**) Babcock Wilson Bevan Viscose* (**TOTAL**) *Pigments Collis Truck Pfleiderer Facts* (**MESS!**)

12

Washing Down

Harry spoke first. 'My goodness. That is quite a sight, Tommy.'

Idzi burst out laughing. 'What the hell mate, yer a right state. Hey, that rhymes!'

Tommy stepped out of the drum. 'Shut it, Idzi. It's the last rehearsal tonight. Maureen'll completely kill me if I turn up looking like this.'

Idzi started crooning: 'Got you... under her thumb.'

Naseem held his laughter, though barely. 'Tommy, I am finding you a boiler suit and gumboots. And there are filter cloths on the shelf for the *saaf kurnay kay liyaay.*'

'Come again?'

'Sorry, for the wiping down.' Naseem nodded. 'They are good for this.'

'What wiping down? What're they good for?'

'Tommy, first there's the *washing* down,' Harry explained.

Tommy tried to squeeze the liquid from the cloth of his trousers. 'Look at my clothes, for God's sake! And look at my hands now! They'll think I've been fighting or something.'

Idzi strutted around the pigment drums. 'Why would they think that, then?'

'Shut it Idzi.'

'It will not be washing off,' Naseem confirmed.

'Not at all?'

Idzi laughed. 'Don't be thick. Just because it's you that's done it doesn't mean pigments isn't permanent.'

'Tommy, we have met your parents once,' Harry said before turning to his brother. '*Sab theek thaak hoe jai ga akhir main Tommy, main tumhare maan baap ko janta hoon aur wo bohut acchay hain.*'

Naseem said, 'Your parents, they are OK.'

'What's that got to do with anything?'

Harry went to find the hose. 'First we will need to wash you down, yes.'

Idzi wiped the tears from his cheeks and honked like a donkey. 'What's it feel like mate, paddling in that? I won't be trying it for myself I'm telling you.'

Naseem arrived with a bundle of old filter cloths and Tommy pulled a face. 'Bit scummy aren't they?'

'They have been washed. You can wrap your shoes to carry them home too. Are you on your bicycle? The clothes, they are only for throwing away.'

'Throwing away? Only? I can't go around barefoot and buff naked.'

'The filter cloths are good for drying down afterwards,' Naseem said.

'Fantastic invention, filter cloths, eh!' Tommy said.

'I will bring a boiler suit now.'

'Can't wait. Sorry,' Tommy called after Naseem, knowing that with mates like Idzi it would be impossible to keep news of the spill from Mr P and everyone else.

Tommy removed each item of clothing much more slowly than if he'd been stripping off in the communal showers after a match, and Idzi leered at his bruises. 'So you *have* been in a fight. Who was it this time?'

Tommy concentrated on the sight of Harry dragging the hose and signalling for Idzi to turn the tap.

At first he was grateful that Harry was trying to aim the hose whilst averting his gaze from the lower part of his body, but the embarrassment actually made it worse because the jet of water kept going off kilter, extending the process.

Then again, he'd be staring at the fight marks, wouldn't he!

Tommy shuddered, not from the coldness of the water but the realisation of how much this mistake had cost his standing with Sunehri's family, not to mention the expense of buying a new set of work clothes. His shoes, once they'd dried out, he'd whack on a few layers of polish, but... he watched Naseem chuck everything else into an industrial size bin.

Eventually Harry motioned for Idzi to switch off the hose and Tommy looked down at his stained feet and legs. 'What was the use of that?'

Harry gave a small smile. 'The liquid pigment is gone. The colour will wear off gradually.'

'Thanks anyway Harry.'

'Let's have a go.' Idzi grabbed one of the dry filter cloths and began attacking Tommy's bare behind.

Tommy shoved him away. 'Leave off! There isn't even any pigment there.'

'Talk about ungrateful. I was only trying to help, wasn't I.'

'Oh yeah?'

51

Idzi pointed at Harry. 'Remove the top layer of skin, that's what he said.'

Tommy sneered. 'Strange, I didn't hear that. Haven't you work to do?'

Idzi began rolling pigment drums away so that the whole area could be hosed down. 'You're the one who's interrupted my work, and too much of a show-off to give a barneys that's what you are, O'Reilly.'

'The Cakewash showers are quiet and there is hot water, yes,' Harry said before returning to his paperwork.

Tommy finished drying in silence, grateful that Jacko wasn't a witness. Maybe not for much longer.

He needed to get out of here!

13

Effects of Light

Naseem handed Tommy a boiler suit and gumboots. 'We have lost some of the red pigment from that drum. It is my dibs to take the next drum home, so we will be collecting the rainwater sooner not later.'

'A water butt for Mrs Butt?' Idzi joked. Then he looked extremely sheepish. 'Did I really say that?'

Tommy shook his head. 'Yes you did.'

'Idzi, I will not be telling my wife a word of it.'

'Sorry, Naseem. I really am.'

'Bye now, Idzi,' Tommy said, as he shoved his legs down the coarse, baggy tubes of the boiler suit. He did the front opening up, stopping at the last buttonhole before the neck, aware that even appalling pieces of clothing had a wrong and a right way of wearing them. A belt might have helped. He stepped into the ill-fitting boots and thought of Sunehri one pelting day last winter, walking across the park wearing her dad's wellies, coming to meet him by the pond. Then the realisation he'd be turning up to a rehearsal in a joker's costume filled him with panic, and cycling home in gumboots wasn't going to be a cinch either. But he must, just must, keep his eye on the job.

'Naseem, any chance of getting me a small sample of that red and bringing it up, straight off?'

'That is no problem. You have not seen enough for one day?'

Tommy grabbed his parcel of shoes and tried a smile. Calling up his map of the factory, he realised that if he took the steps at the far end of the building he'd be able to pass along the ends of the spinning machines without stoking up too much notice, and from there take a direct route to the showers.

In the showers he discovered that the sole purpose of getting drenched for a third time was to wash off the flecks of filter cloth that had stuck to his body during the wiping down.

Tommy chose the only towel that didn't smell rancid and winced at the sensation of yet another rough piece of material grating his skin. Once dressed, he made his hair as decent as possible without access to a comb, and left for the Lab.

He opened the door cautiously and walked to his bench.

Melville arrived on Tommy's side of the bench like a returned ping-pong ball. 'Aw, Tommy Red, look at the spatters across that handsome face!'

Tommy blanked him. When his stained shoes rolled out of their filter cloth wrappings and landed at Victor Hesketh's feet, the Spectre smiled.

Jean raised the shoes by their laces as though she was dangling rats' tails. 'Tell Aunty Jean all about it.'

'You're not old enough to be my aunty and you obviously know already.' Tommy's jaw was set. 'I've work to do.'

The Spectre had so far stayed silent. Tommy could see him looking in the direction of Mr P's office. Their manager was safely distracted on the phone and Tommy prepared himself for the attack.

'If Tommy Red's been injured,' Victor droned, 'we should be showing sympathy, not calling him nasty names.'

Jean said, 'Look at thee 'ands!'

Tommy looked at his hands. 'Suppose I've seen them more... flesh-coloured.'

Victor tutted. 'You know Jean, that broad Lancashire accent is starting to grate with me.'

Jean didn't give up easily. 'Ee, where's the rest of thee togs?'

Melville caught hold of one of Tommy's gaping trouser legs. 'And what have you got on under here?'

'If you really want to know, absolutely nowt.'

Victor's eyebrows disappeared under his home-cut fringe.

Tommy was left with the feeling that he'd got off lightly with Victor, and that the others had more than made up for it.

When Naseem walked in carrying a sample jar with a dark liquid swilling round, Red 1175-62, Tommy immediately placed the two trial spinnings from the previous day side-by-side in the light box. 'I like the look of this, Naseem!'

He used his judgement to make a revised recipe that included a small quantity of the new red, and took it straight down to the Duracol department.

It was late afternoon by the time the new sample spinning was delivered by Vivian. 'All right, Tommy? That is some tale we've been hearing, and none of it will be true I suppose.'

He liked Vivian. 'Number one, I'm fine. Number two, I'm not discussing it.'

As soon as Mr Postlethwaite was free, Tommy went to see him about the shade. The manager used the light box first, then stood with his back to the window in his office and examined the yarn with the light coming over his shoulder. 'I'm checking the effect proper daylight has on the shade, compared to the artificial light in the box. See that?'

Tommy nodded.

'Not to worry about this spillage thing, lad,' the manager said as he placed all the trial shades next to the customer's example shade. 'I can tell from your face you're still not content with the match.'

Tommy went off to tweak the percentages, using a little more red in the recipe. Soon he was heading full-pelt for the Caves, aware that if he went fast enough he wouldn't catch the demeaning comments thrown at him. Since the pigment needed to be weighed, the viscose collected from the Spinning department, then pigmented and de-aerated, and it took about three hours to prepare the yarn, the next trial spinning wouldn't be ready until tomorrow morning. Despite his mess-up, there was enough time in the schedule. Just.

He left the slip of paper with the recipe on the desk in the Duracol office, feeling grateful that the place was empty.

When the siren signalled the end of the day, Tommy packed up quickly. Maureen would be narked if he was late again. He launched himself into the stair-turns and as he arrived at the entrance to the men's canteen he pulled up sharp.

14

Tickling the Ivories

A giant poster had been pinned to the wall, and there was another by the opening to the women's canteen:

~ COME AND SEE ~

"Happy Cavalcade"

presented by Atherton's Drama Society
A summer musical directed, produced & choreographed by
Maureen Copton with accompaniment by Harry Manzoor

Thursday the 6th of July 7.30pm

Tommy O'Reilly as Ernest Markham & Johnny Winterbottom
& his mother & his Doctor (a comical number)

Doris Smith as Henrietta Brown

Chorus members - Jean Crossthwaite (solo: "Cum Saturday"),

Chas Chaney, John Houghton, Sheila Mullaney

Stand-in - Bonnie Alston   Costumes and props - Bonnie Alston

Tickets - 50p (cheap at the price!) Programmes - 10p

Both available at the Women's Canteen entrance on the night

Design & photos - Dicky N.   Printing - Stanleys, 3, High Street, Preston

Tommy had seen smaller versions pinned on notice-boards round the factory, but at that size! The poster would look *bohut khoob* brilliant in his room. He'd nick one straight after the performance.

Every year Atherton's Drama Society staged a Christmas play, and a musical performance before workers took their summer holidays. Summer 1972 was to be a bundle of favourite songs about Lancashire's past - cotton mills not viscose, which was the future. The music had been strung together by Harry and Maureen, and Maureen had come up with a loose story about two young people falling in love that only required a small cast. Tommy would be kissing Doris Smith from the General Office, leading lady Henrietta to his Ernest. Not his first choice, obviously.

Dicky N had produced the posters between devising an automated transfer system for the steep presses, with valves replacing the need for the operatives to sling sheets over the wall on to the churn slide. Tommy looked at his watch. He couldn't even get to rehearsals on time.

'I much prefer the plays,' Doris was saying as Tommy entered the canteen to the general buzz of a company assembling. He'd think of Olivier and try not to squirm if Maureen directed them to rehearse the lovers' kiss again.

'Me too,' said Sheila. 'It's a bit clearer what to wear in a play, when there's, dare I say it, a proper storyline? Though of course Maureen's done a grand job as usual.'

'I wouldn't necessarily go that far,' Doris was saying, when she noticed Tommy. 'Your character doesn't wear overalls!'

Everyone stared.

'Which character are you referring to?' Tommy asked. 'I'm playing more than one.'

'A dapper young gent like Ernest wouldn't be seen dead looking like that,' Doris said.

Chas raised his hand. 'I heard the sorry tale, and no doubt this radical re-interpretation at the eleventh hour is the result of that unfortunate accident?'

Tommy listened as the company continued their commentary on the pigment spill. Feeling pleased that Jean wasn't joining in, he distracted himself with a dissection of the workers from the General Office, who were the mainstay of the group. In his less kind moments, like now, Tommy saw little connection between the membership and their acting talent. The company had their share of war medals, never mentioned and he'd found out by chance through Mr P, so he couldn't help feeling disappointed that acting was seen as something completely separate from real life. He shoved his stained fingers deep into his deep pockets and tried to keep quiet.

'He's blushing now,' said Sheila. 'I suppose that's something.'

'Typical of you, Tommy O'Reilly, trying to up-stage everyone.' Doris swivelled round. 'Anyway, it's not all about him. What were we saying earlier about Music Hall as a style of entertainment? I have to say, I do have a soft spot for the *Henrietta's Happy* number. Lyrical. Is that the word?'

'It's a word,' Tommy said, spotting his opportunity. 'Anyway, you would say that - it's your only solo.'

'Doris always shines,' Sheila said.

Tommy couldn't resist. 'How I see it is, Sheila can hold a high note, Chas can hold a low note, John can hold most of the notes in between, Doris has a solo because - remind me why Doris has a solo? Jean has the best...'

The director stomped over. 'No bickering, guys and gals, we've work to do.' Maureen Copton smiled at Tommy. 'You're late. And what are you doing wearing overalls? Even if it were a full dress rehearsal, you seem to have the wrong production.'

The company sniggered and Tommy flicked his quiff. 'They're very comfy, actually.'

'I'll bet they are!' Maureen raised her arms. 'How's about the opening number for our warm-up? See how that one goes.'

Harry was sitting at an upright piano that had been placed to the side of what would become a fully-fledged stage.

'When you're ready, Harry.'

The pianist finished spreading out the sheet music then he played an extended introduction that would give the punters a flavour of the evening's entertainment and a chance to get to their seats. On the director's signal the company entered stage right, male and female alternating arm in arm.

'Women's football team struggling a bit?' Tommy whispered to Sheila.

'You're such a so-and-so! Well, your Mr Murphy, he can't even decide whether to back the men's team on Saturday. And if *he* can't, there's no hope.'

'Ta for that. It's always been Mel's style anyway. He backs within a whisker of closing.'

'Not exactly a vote of confidence is it, not that you'd notice.'

The air stirred nearby. This was Doris, alias Henrietta, flouncing past in her big blue bonnet and twirling a parasol with some skill. As Tommy stepped forward to sing behind Ernest Markham's semi-raised hand, he did a count-up; the same parasol had featured in the last five productions.

> *See the pretty lassie in the big blue bonnet*
> *The big blue bonnet with the pretty flowers on it?*

Doris beamed at Ernest and the chorus sang:

> *Ain't she sweet now,*
> *Don't she look a treat now,*
> *There's not another like her in the whole darned street*
> *Wow!*

Doris waved coquettishly and Tommy took up the line:

> *Hey! Who's the bonny one?*

Followed by Chas and Jean:

> *Isn't she the bonny one!*

The chorus echoed:

> *Such a very bonny one, with her bonnet on...*

Inappropriately, as far as Tommy was concerned, the whole company including Doris kicked up their feet, turned this way and that, rested hands on hips, and worked up a sweat as choreographed until it was time for Tommy to deliver his aside to the empty canteen, still shielding his words from a straining-to-listen Henrietta:

> *You'd bet I'd marry her tomorrow*
> *If it wasn't for the sorrow*
> *That I'd get from the missus back home!*

Here, the chorus tutted in an exaggerated way, supported by Maureen in the hypothetical wings - an incitement for the audience to enter into the Music Hall spirit.

'All together now...' Tommy made a wipe sweep of his arm

to rouse the hundreds of invisible punters. He caught the eye of the pastry chef. 'Come on Danuta, don't be shy now!'

The pastry chef ducked behind the pans and the company rounded off with another belt through. This morphed into a sequence of discordant piano chords that signalled doom after the interval. The chorus walked off, followed by Tommy arm in arm with his new girlfriend.

'All right, loves,' Maureen said. 'I'm quite surprised how well that went, compared to our previous run-through. Now for our second song about bonnets - how did that happen, by the way?'

'Secret Drama Society meetings?' Chas Chaney muttered.

'And they wore a lot of bonnets in those days,' Jean said. 'Before women became emancipated. It was a surprisingly long time ago.'

Tommy knew that Jean was commenting on the portrayal of the female characters. No one else seemed to be bothered.

Next, Doris wandered wistfully about the stage while Jean and John sang in unison:

Mind thi ways, mind thi ways, mi bold bonny lassie,
Watch out for thisself or tha'll soon rue this day,
For he'll have thee to sing to his song if tha'll let him
And dance to the beat of his loom if he may.

Tommy entered, speaking sinuously over the music:

Henrietta's abroad in her Sunday best bonnet,
The blackest, the blackest, the blackest of black,
Trimmed all about...

He paused for a few seconds to check the director's response. Maureen nodded and Tommy continued:

... with one broad silk ribbon, The reddest, the redd...

He'd forgotten Melville's advice about putting base colour on his right cheek. But it looked like he'd got away with it.

The company gathered round for notes. When the director reached the bottom she smiled at Tommy and he thought he was going to hear something positive. 'Take off those wellies!' she said. 'You can't move in them. Honestly!'

The gumboots didn't come off easily because Tommy was in bare feet. The delay added to the director's annoyance. 'Jean's solo next,' Maureen announced. 'Quiet please.'

Jean smiled at Tommy before walking on. There was no accompaniment, and the room was hushed as she made her way to the centre of the space, composed herself, and began singing a song with about twenty verses that got on Tommy's nerves. It ended with:

The morning sun has yet to pass the pall of night
to light the frosty scrawl that Jack did trace
while thou didst sleep.
And mind thi keep a civil tongue, mi lass
and heed thi teacher's way
'Tis time to kiss the shuttle now...

Nearing the side-wall representing off-stage Jean projected a whisper to the room, *'thou can'st play again cum Saturday.'*

Tommy noticed that Clive and the other painters had stopped working and that in the kitchen the choux piping was poised mid-squeeze. There was a loud applause and the director rushed over. 'That's the best you've ever sung it. Absolutely gorgeous.'

Though he would have preferred never to hear either, he definitely favoured Maureen's office voice to her luvvie one.

It was his solo next.

15

Johnny Winterbottom
(aka Ernest Markham)

Before Ernest was to be killed off in the land of the Happy Cavalcade he had to half-speak and half-sing a ditty about a tragic character called Johnny Winterbottom. Doubts had been expressed at the planning stage, not only by Tommy, but the song had been voted in because it guaranteed a few laughs - at his expense.

Tommy marched on, slipped and fell. 'It's mashed potato or something!' he complained. This wasn't part of the script.

Maureen dashed over with an embroidered hanky. 'Keep going love. Harry's waiting with his rippling chords.'

The company watched Tommy studiously wipe the soles of his feet then offer the hanky back to Maureen, who refused it. 'Give it a wash first, there's a pretty.'

Tommy thought of their encounter last summer, how he'd rejected Maureen's advances. When Harry repeated the run-in for a fourth time, he stuffed the hanky into his pocket and began recounting the sad tale of Mr Winterbottom. It came out sounding more monotone than intended:

Oh, Johnny were a fighting lad
Not gentle like a lamb,
But he got his comeuppance, didn't he,
the day he mixed wi a tram.

Harry played a few bars and Tommy geared up for the voice of Johnny's mother.

'Oh, Johnny lad,' his mother cried,
'whatever hast t'done?
Tha's gone and lost a nether limb
And now tha's only one.'

Tommy blushed. This was excruciating. Reverting to Ernest Markham's voice, he continued:

So, Johnny and his leg were parted
by a distance of some feet
and it were obvious to everyone
that ne'er the twain would meet.

He paused for audience laughter, but since the players and stage crew had heard the joke a few times he had to use his imagination.

They took him off to th'ospital
t'see what could be done,
Johnny went in th'ambulance first
And t'left leg followed on.
T'doctor looked at Johnny
and then he looked at t'leg...

At this point Tommy prepared to impersonate the doctor from the perspective and voice-box of Ernest:

'... Ah I can see nowt else for it, lad,
it'll have t'be a peg.'

65

Tommy looked across at Harry and remembered just in time to revert to the pure Ernest character for his next lines:

Now, although he'd got a peg leg,
it didn't cause him bovver...
Johnny simply dotted one
and then he carried t'other!

Harry banged on the piano case to signify the points at which Johnny Winterbottom's wooden leg hit the floor. Tommy had always found this part distracting.

You know... err...
Oh, it isn't nice t'call folks names
But... still it seemed t'some
that Johnny Dot and Carry One
bested Johnny Chilly Bum!

Tommy took a step forward and called out to the serving hatch, 'That's *Winterbottom* to you!'

In the silence that ensued Maureen walked over. 'Wonderful SP as expected, Tommy, though it's a tricky ending, a bit of a tongue-twister isn't it. I'd say work on it at home.'

For safety, Tommy kept his mouth shut.

The director gathered everyone round again. 'Now Tommy, are you secure with your tragic end and your reactions to your lover's reactions in the summerhouse?'

Everyone looked at him.

'*I'm* fine,' Doris cut in. 'Wouldn't know about the show-off.'

Tommy sent her an ironic kiss.

'So,' continued Maureen, '*My Old Man* we'll leave for the night or you'll get stale. The audience will carry it anyway. Okey-dokey, thanks everyone. See you all here an hour before

66

the start, if not before round and about the place.'

The company thanked her back, then Maureen thanked everyone individually, adding 'love' to their names. To Tommy she said, 'Don't be late, and clean your fingernails and make sure you slap plenty of flesh-coloured base on that cheek.'

So she had noticed. Tommy picked up a programme. 'Not bad, are they?'

'Sorry?' Maureen was looking flushed.

He held out the programme. 'Reet good actually, as my mam always says.'

'Yes, all credit to Dicky on the text and design. Same design, different show, that's all right. He got them printed up at...'

'Stanleys?' Tommy said, wondering why he was lingering.

'Lovely. Now, that's the worst patch, on your right cheek. Number 9 to us thespians.' She sounded like Hattie Jacques playing matron.

'Bye Harry,' Tommy called.

Harry waved. 'Tommy is quite something,' he said, when Maureen came to help with the music. 'A good lad, when you...'

'Look beyond the swagger?'

Harry nodded. 'Maybe, Maureen. Where is Bonnie tonight?'

'Putting the finishing touches to a few costumes. Seen the state of his nails though, Harry? I missed the exact reason - I was out of the office today.'

Harry didn't snitch, and instead concentrated on slotting the music into a cardboard wallet with the words *Abbu's Show* scrawled on the front. 'Tahira made this wallet, for her daddy.'

Maureen smiled. 'It's lasted well. How many years since you joined the company, Harry?'

Harry smoothed the corner where the cardboard was beginning to fluff. 'Tahira, she was seventeen last weekend.' He paused. 'You know she is getting married?'

'In Preston?'

'Her husband will be in Pakistan, so she is going there, yes.'

They walked and picked up the bonnets and other discarded props on the way.

'Her little brother and sister will miss her,' Maureen said.

'Umair and Yasir, yes they will, and the girls in the Coning. Tahira is happy with her decision.'

They dropped the things into the box and carried it together to the designated cupboard.

'There's still lots to do, Harry, and how lost would we be if Mr Atherton didn't allocate money for the set materials and joiners and painters, not forgetting the leckies and the Heavy Gang!'

Harry nodded.

'Well, congratulations to your daughter and Mrs Manzoor. Please say, from me.'

Harry smiled. 'Thank you.'

Out on the road, Tommy's gumboots had slipped off the pedals a dozen times before he had a plan. He'd ferret out the hard bristle brush his mam used for scrubbing the front step. He wasn't sure about using it on his face, but it was worth a try. Mostly he thought about Sunehri and telling her his version of the truth.

16

Secrets

Next day Tommy pedalled furiously to work in a borrowed shirt and trousers. The clothes weren't too bad a fit since he and his dad were both tall and skinny, but Tommy wasn't too happy about the shoes. The left shoe was a definite black, while the right one still veered towards mauve after three coats of wax.

At the gatehouse Mr Embley gave him the briefest of nods and Tommy wondered how many years it would take to earn a full salute.

He made some progress with the special shade between helping with other urgent jobs, and for once he avoided rather than looked for fights with Victor. He left it as late as possible to try and see Sunehri too. When he did approach the opening to the Coning department he was forced to speak to Doris, to avoid coinciding with Alfonso Giorgio.

He tried twice more in the afternoon. No sign of her.

At five-thirty exactly Tommy packed away his things and said goodnight to Mr P.

'See you tomorrow, lad,' the manager called. 'Don't be a worrit. Almost there.'

As Tommy took the overgrown footpaths on the edge of the site his mind wandered to the last Christmas holidays, when they'd been apart for far too long. On his return to work he'd gone looking for somewhere to chuck a glass phial he'd cracked - he wasn't going to lose his clean record - and a bird flying up from a hedge had caught his attention. He'd taken a closer look and discovered the disused storeroom, similar in size to a shed.

'Tommy?'

Sunehri's face appeared. '*Mujhay tum bohut yaad aye tthey!*'

They slipped inside and she shoved the bolt across.

'I missed you too,' he said, feeling awkward.

'It is different. Has someone been here Tommy?'

'Like it?'

Sunehri took her time to walk the little circuit and admire the book-lined floor with its candle at the centre. 'A palace.'

'I feel sorry for the Royal Family.'

'Me too, but I did always want to be a princess.'

Tommy shifted from one foot to the other. 'You're strange. Spent too long playing with your dolls or something.'

Sunehri avoided Tommy when he lurched forwards for a kiss. 'And I am sorry for you,' she said, as she went to sit in the middle of the floor. It was still uncomfortable. She didn't say. She tentatively stroked the bubble that had blistered on her index finger, feeling resentful he hadn't asked her about it yet.

Tommy sat close by and passed his hand across the floor. 'I sorted through those old factory manuals.'

'I like it.' Then she frowned. 'What has happened to your cheek? It looks sore. Was it that fight?'

He didn't want to talk about the fight or the accident. Maybe she was playing games, pretending she hadn't heard about the pigment spill. It was unlikely, but then again he wasn't aware of her ever having lied to him. He lit the candle and with his hand he made the shape of a chunky shadow with horns. 'Have devils in your religion do you? And hell?' His shape reared up against the wall.

'Devils?' she asked. '*Shaitaan?*'

His hand writhed grotesquely before falling out of the light. 'That was you being crushed to a pulp in a Pfleiderer!'

'You sound like my enemy, Tommy. Why are we playing shadows again?'

'I thought you liked it, from when you were a girl.'

Sunehri pointed to his bright red fingernails. 'Is this Devil?'

He shifted his weight and glanced the candle flame. 'I brought a torch, after you got that burn. The candle though, I think it's more... romantic.' He glanced at his torch, still tucked in by the door. 'You won't be able to get this shape, either.'

Sunehri looked away. 'Stop it, Tommy. You are pleased with yourself. I do not know why. Anyway, you are far too large to make a shadow of your whole body against the wall. Look - out of focus.'

He motioned for her to come and sit between his legs.

For a while she resisted. When at last she shuffled into position she needed to crane her neck to follow the soft pencil smudges of freckles that stretched from the bridge of his nose all the way across his cheeks. 'I saw the posters. Your name is big, next to Doris.'

'I really don't want to talk about her. I don't mind telling you about this, though. See, for the Guild there's to be a flag with a golden-coloured background and maybe a picture of a lamb lying down, well more like sitting down, with two capital letter Ps on the flag it's holding.' Tommy crooked his arm as though it were in a sling, to represent how a lamb might clamp a flagpole under its front leg. 'See, the lamb's carrying a flag, and this flag has a smaller picture of a lamb carrying a flag, and that flag has an even smaller picture of a lamb carrying... I made that last bit up.'

'You look funny! A flag, *chota jhanda?*'

'PP for Princeps Pacis, Prince of Peace. Not Proud Preston - loads of people make that mistake. And did you know, they don't sell flags on the Flag Market. I think that's potty. They sell pots once a year though, so...'

She laughed. 'I have lived here since I was five. The ground is made of stone flags. They sometimes sell flags, when there's a big football game.' Sunehri shifted awkwardly on the glossy flooring. 'Don't they?'

Tommy didn't respond.

'Try and guess what my Uncle Harry's name means,' she said.

'Barry?'

'I mean his surname.'

'Manglewurzle?'

'Stop being silly all the time, Tommy. "Manzoor" means admired, or approved, or granted... or chosen.'

'Anything else? Isn't that a bit greedy?'

'Uncle Harry is very modest. He requires one compliment every minute or so, that's all.'

'Harry's like that at home is he, with the compliments? I'm shocked.'

'Since Tahira is leaving to be married soon...'

'That surprises me about Harry. I suppose I could test him

72

out. Hey, how about you give me loads of compliments now, so I can get some good ideas for what to say when I'm conducting my research on your uncle? They'll need to be authentic compliments - you know, relevant to me too.'

'You are trouble Tommy, and vain. *Mujhay jana hay.* I need to be home early. Maa asked many questions last time.'

Instead of leaving, they fell into kissing.

'I will try and talk to her,' Sunehri whispered. 'Maybe Abbu, but I will not see him this year. Perhaps I can save up enough money for a long phone call.'

Tommy fought the impulse to lie fully with her. He sensed they both wanted it. He knew it would be a mistake.

'We do not have that kind of money,' she said quietly.

He couldn't imagine talking to his parents about Sunehri, yet she was the only person who mattered. As his eyes fixed on the undulating lines of the wood, the details of his life fell away - work, his ongoing fight with Fons, even football - everything was small compared to her. And she came with secrets, secrets they'd made together. He knew it wasn't possible to sustain secrets for a lifetime, and no matter how many ways he came at it, the situation wasn't right.

Tommy broke apart. *He couldn't stand this!*

Sunehri was watching his face. 'I do not like to ask what you are thinking.'

He moved the candle closer to the wall, brought his thumbs together and separated the fingers until they were like feathers flapping languorously up, down, up, down.

'What is this shape?' she asked.

'You, flying. Escaping maybe. I don't know, do I.'

freckles across his cheeks darkened.

dark skin became darker too. '*Chiriya, main teray say piyaar karti hoon,*' she said. 'I love you, Bird.'

'*Chiriya, main teray...*' Tommy began. 'Yes, a bird shadow.'

'*Chiriyaan* - two birds flying together?' she asked.

'No,' he said.

A gust of wind burst through a crack and snuffed the candle out. Although he knew his eyes would adjust to the darkness, he closed them so that he might see her more clearly.

Sunehri lit the candle again. 'Is that true? Not us together?'

Tommy watched her face flicker.

After a few moments she stood up. '*Mujhay jana hay.* I have to go.'

'I haven't asked you about your finger. Can I look? Don't go yet. Why do you have to go?' He stretched his hand out for her to take.

'Ask me *why* in my language, Tommy. You are lazy.'

Tommy tried to dredge up the words to say that he didn't understand. He became muddled. '*Mujhay samaj nah...*'

'You do,' she interrupted in a dry voice, then walked out.

When they were standing on the path, Tommy leant against the wonky door. One part of him wanted to shut off their den from every living creature. Another part of him wanted to tear away the bushes and put a sign up for tourists.

Sunehri ran towards the gate and he watched the beautiful *chiriya* flying from him.

17

Break a Leg

It was the day of the show. Tommy waved at Nicolas in the gatehouse and reckoned he'd be down in the Duracol department ten minutes early. He would tell Sunehri about Maureen Copton when it felt right. Nothing had happened, not really, but there was some history.

The window hatch slid open and Tommy stopped his bike. Nicolas Martens was on earlies, so he was able to tell Tommy what had happened during the night. From the gatehouse Mr Embley had seen smoke rising at the south-east corner of the site a short time after his night shift had begun at 10pm. The chief commissionaire had taken the rough paths towards Water Softening. Being younger than Mr Embley and not having worked at Atherton's as long, Nicolas had not been aware of a wooden storeroom that had become hidden by established rhododendron bushes. As Mr Embley had approached the structure there was an explosion, probably old canisters and/or petrol tanks, he thought. The blaze was not large and he had called the fire steward, who had attended the scene. The remainder of the combustible materials had been removed and no further action was necessary because that part of the site was not frequented by workers. It was all in the log report. The few odds and sods worth salvaging Mr Embley had acquired for the gatehouse.

Tommy noticed Nicolas scrutinising him, and he struggled to contain his feelings. He dug his fingernails into his palms. 'See you later,' he said, trying to sound casual. He resolved to find a new place to be alone with Sunehri. More than one. There were more storage spaces on the massive site than you could count, and he hadn't even looked into the possibility of the elevated gantries where the electrics were laid.

Tommy checked himself in a window. His hair looked fine. His cheek felt tender - he'd put it down to a new razor if anyone asked.

Naseem spotted Tommy and approached with a spun cake. 'What a shade!'

Tommy took possession of the wound yarn. 'Thanks Naseem. Worth decorating your floor with?'

Naseem rolled his head. 'I am not sure I will go that far.'

Jacko rushed by and nearly knocked the yarn from Tommy's hands. 'Bloody bus, sorry mate! Stood waiting ages, I was.'

'Hiya, Jacko. Usual excuse. Don't know why you bother - nobody believes you any more.' Tommy didn't have time for small-talk. His heart was racing. 'I'll be down later Naseem, if it needs adjusting. I'll check with Mr P. Hopefully it can go to the Cakewash later today.'

'Tommy, any time for you.'

Jacko backtracked to take a proper look at the trial spinning. 'Whey, that's a one!' He patted Tommy on the head. 'I'll come with you, stop off at the...' Jacko whistled his signature tune for the men's toilets.

'The price of that pigment, Jacko - I checked it in the book.'

Jacko grabbed the cake. 'It's a stunner. Will Mr P go for it?'

'There's no other pigment will give us the shade I've got in my head. It's what the Mayor wanted, but better.'

'Not another one of your visions.'

Tommy retrieved the cake. 'Anyway, it'll only take a smidgeon so it doesn't matter what it costs.'

Jacko thumped his friend on the back, a bit too hard on purpose. 'Serious, aren't you.'

'Geddoff! This is the discovery of a lifetime.'

'Oh shame - think I'll have to stick my head down the toilet.' Jacko leant into the door, releasing a faint whiff of bleach with undertones of urine.

'That's friends,' Tommy said.

He arrived at his bench in seconds, unravelled some yarn from the inside of the new cake and twisted the golden-coloured threads into a swatch, tying off the ends.

Mr Postlethwaite walked in. 'Tommy lad, I was going to ask if you were all right cycling home last night? Managed to keep that boiler suit from flapping in the chain did you?'

Salaam was the word that came to Tommy, but by thinking his greeting in Urdu he failed to say anything at all.

Frank laughed. 'You've obviously other things on your mind!'

'See Mr Postlethwaite, I know the pigment's a bit dear, well, to be honest really dear, but we're only using 0.02%.'

Frank raised an eyebrow. 'Which pigment's that?'

'Red 1175-62. A tiny bit's all we need.'

'Never heard of it. Sounds ancient. Made in 1962 probably. Clue's in the number.'

Tommy thrust the swatch of unwashed yarn into his manager's hand. It smelt of acid.

Frank was bowled over by what he saw.

'Look, Mr Postlethwaite.'

'I am looking.'

The manager went to his office and turned to examine the shade with the window light shining directly onto it. Tommy watched carefully.

'You know Tommy, what's most impressed me is your taking the initiative.'

'But what do you think of the shade, Mr Postlethwaite?'

'Well, we can't tell until it's washed and dried. Get it down to the Cakewash and then we'll have another look. If we still think it's a stunner then we'll ask the Mayor for his opinion.'

Shukriya and bloody *bohut khoob*. Tommy thought.

'We need to keep these Guild traditions going, don't we lad. I'll have a look at the costings later.'

Tommy left the processing order with Idzi, then his impulse was to detour and ask Sunehri if she'd look out for the final shade when it came through. She might even wind the thread on a cone herself... but he was running too fast. They'd see each other tonight anyway, hopefully exchange a few words. She'd forgive him for the Johnny Winterbottom.

She'd love him!

Because of spending so much time on the special order, Tommy's job list had grown enormous. He focused hard all day and didn't collect a single snide remark from Victor.

An hour before the siren, Mr P came over. 'Better scootle. Can't keep our Maureen waiting.'

His manager's use of the word "our" struck Tommy as strange, but he didn't think any more about it, and he left the laboratory feeling that life couldn't get any better - except that it might be quite good to know that Sunehri Saleem loved him exactly the same amount, if not more.

'Break a leg.' This was the Spectre's voice, and he probably meant it. For the first time in his life Tommy felt a bit sorry for Victor Hesketh, who as far as he knew had never had a girlfriend, and he must be over thirty years old by now.

18

Gone and Left Him

So here he was exactly a week after the show, his mind in turmoil, his heart racing like a babby's. Instead of working, Tommy was staring at the knots in the bench, and although the wood seemed solid, he might as well be falling into an abyss.

Mr P came in with Harry Manzoor, and Tommy heard Harry say something when the pull-back banged his ankle - fire safety regulations that had caught Tommy out more than once.

He watched his manager check some paperwork and made sure he was looking down when Harry was leaving. He mustn't, just mustn't catch the eye of Sunehri Saleem's uncle.

Frank Postlethwaite had always given Tommy guidance, saved him from scrapes, calmed the situation when he'd shown Victor too much cheek in the early days; well, some things never changed. He might have stayed an assistant without Frank...

'How's it going, lad? That little job?'

Tommy's face dropped, although his feelings towards his manager were warm. 'Mr Postlethwaite, I... I've a few ideas.'

'Good. Tell me about them.'

The truth was, Tommy had nothing.

To his relief, the phone rang and Frank Postlethwaite went to answer it. 'Sorry, we'll talk later.'

Names, words, expressions, the *way* she said things, being patient yet insistent, encouraging him, teaching him, loving him. It was only questions that filled his mind now.

Kya haal hay? How's it going, Tommy?

Mujhay naheen patta. How do I know?

Confusions to answer confusions.

All he had were those *other* words, how they made him feel.

And the factory.

The mental map he'd made in his first few months here, the locations of goods lifts, the many storage rooms and offices, the toilets and all the other places you could get away with smoking, as long as the Collis truck was laden with boxes, flasks, filters, anything, he could go where he wanted. Collect and deliver, find out about the people and processes, brush it off when he was accused of being a nosy sort, be the best he could be. It had worked. It had all been fine.

Then last autumn Sunehri had arrived. It was the week after her seventeenth birthday, his nineteenth on the same day. She'd started at Atherton's on the point of his promotion and this had posed problems when he'd least expected them. His new job was an opportunity he'd gladly taken. It didn't involve a Collis or any valid reasons to travel between the Lab and the Coning department on a regular basis. The brown-tiled corridors that wiggled like liquorice, lifts, walkways, they used to lead to her. She wasn't there any more.

These last six months the hundreds of new points he'd created on his map were about the times they'd found to be together, minutes caught, seconds snatched, everything snatched. That was all right. It was all right. And finding the den at New Year, well, that had become the sole place on his map.

Today his map was blank.

He couldn't believe she'd gone. Gone and left him.

'Feeling under the weather, lad?' The manager pulled up a stool and Tommy shoved his shaking hands into the pockets of his lab coat. It was a uniform he'd always felt proud to wear. Now he wasn't worthy of it.

Frank said softly, 'I suppose thinking doesn't require your hands, so that's fine, for a bit at least.'

'I'm on to it Mr P.' Tommy felt like his life was over.

The phone interrupted again. 'Everyone's finishing up before they're away off for their break.' Frank Postlethwaite strode to his office to answer before three rings. "Pride" Tommy called it. "Standards" was his manager's word.

I know who I am. *Meera naam Tommy O'Reilly hay.* I'm Tommy O'Reilly. Mr P was straight up, kind. It was nice that he'd noticed. It wasn't enough. Shine to your fullest potential. So what was wrong with that? Tommy knew that he could never stack up. What good had he ever done?

Victor caught Tommy's attention. 'Under the weather? Well-cut? Lots of ways of saying it, aren't there. Hung over, there's another one. I suppose it feels the same no matter what name you give it.'

Tommy stood up. 'I don't remember saying anything to you.'

'You have been unusually quiet this week.'

Melville nodded. 'Eh, suffering like that at your age.'

'Mel, you're not more than four years older than Tommy,' Jean said. 'And I was generous not to apply terms to you with that splitting headache brought on by choice.'

'Very well expressed, Jean.' Melville whistled a long note and returned to his production figures in the ledger.

Tommy stared at a beaker on the bench. It was beautifully curved, a work of art, understated. He'd washed that flask carefully hundreds of times. Now all he could hear was a point of impact followed by hundreds of tiny notes ringing from a waterfall of glass. He looked beyond his feet to the herringbone floor. It'd be a pain to sweep up, like confetti after a wedding.

'Hear my song, Violetta...' Jean was on her way to the darkroom humming his grandma's hoovering tune.

'Need some help?' Tommy asked her.

'Not really. I'm only checking the holes for blockages, seeing if we need a jet change.'

'You've persuaded me,' he said.

Inside the darkroom Tommy watched Jean position a piece of fine string on the bench-top, then lay across it the amount of yarn she thought she'd need for an order that had just come in. Once the lengths of yarn were straight enough, she brought the ends of the string together and pushed them through the last of eight holes in the metal strip. Finally, she pulled the yarn through, using the string loop.

'How many threads in there?' he asked.

'About seventy, what you'd use for ladies' tights. Too much yarn and it'll fall out of the hole when you cut the ends, too little and the yarn will drag some of the threads - then it won't work when you take a photo of the cross-section.'

Tommy smelt her skin. It was un-perfumed like Sunehri's. 'Tight fit isn't it, in the hole.'

Jean laughed. 'I don't think you meant to say that, did you?'

'Sorry.' The darkroom forgave his embarrassment.

Jean used a razor blade to shear off the thread ends on each side of the metal strip, leaving a small wad in the hole, then she adjusted the light on the microscope so that the image of the yarn's cross-section would project onto the bench.

Tommy was beginning to sweat in the small space. 'Can I have a go at the focusing?'

'Be my guest.'

It took him a few tries before he was ready to switch off the orange lamp.

In the dark, Jean positioned a piece of orthochromatic photographic paper under the microscope and switched the lamp on again.

'Jean, how do you know how long to leave the microscope light on, for the exposure? I suppose it's different depending on the denier? I watched Mel last week, forgot to ask him.'

'No it isn't,' she said. 'It's the same every time - about.'

'About? Helpful.'

'No need to be sniffy with me. Five seconds then.'

Tommy wondered how he'd managed to get to a state where he considered trial and error a bad thing. 'I bet you don't know the deniers you get for the number of holes in the spinning machine jets. I do, off by heart.'

'Enlighten me.'

Tommy took her at her word. 'Well, the lowest is 75.'

'Never!' she said. 'There's no need to state the obvious.'

'Am I in the way?'

'No, it's fine, Tommy. Just hurry up and finish what you were wanting to tell me about jet holes.'

Tommy smiled. 'So, 75 denier is made with 18 holes in the head of the jet, 100 denier is either 20 holes or 30 depending on the size of the hole, 120 denier is 24 holes, 150 is 50, 200 is 40, 250 is 50 and top whack, 300 denier is 50 holes.'

'Well, thank goodness for that.' Jean continued with the photographic process and neither of them spoke again.

19

Chiriya

I saw the crow, a *chiriya* flying sharp and black. Was I seeing it from the corner of your eye rather than my own? What else could it be, since I wasn't there?

Well I, or you, saw the bird settle on the hard ground. Its breath steamed like a human's, too large a mist for a crow-sized pair of lungs.

A desolate place without fire or women working the fire. No men raising heat through irons or the carrying of logs, no children playing on the ice. No sounds except the ice in the air, insistent, anaesthetised, crystals making the ending seem easy when it should be hard.

The world should always notice when love is lost and death is waved in like a friend or neighbour, or both. I sense that we both agree.

I don't know for sure.

When you turn and smile beyond my knowledge of you, my breath is gone. Do you know me from somewhere? I don't really know you. Where have you seen me?

I'm looking at you from the side.

Just look at you with your smile. How wonderful to smile like that. I will try it, the way you're looking at me now.

20

Lullaby

Tommy realised he was alone. He hurried through to the laboratory and was met by a glare from Victor, the lamps from the cabinet casting an ethereal glow over his pale skin. Tommy returned the glare. He was sick of the Spectre, and sicker of himself.

He picked up the two-by-four backing card wound with the latest viscose sample and stroked his fingertip across its filaments, as glossy as real silk. He needed to find a name for the new shade, that was all, something for the Shade Book and the customer, and then he'd be done with it.

But he couldn't concentrate.

Say if he blew the factory up, there'd be no option but to live without her. He could amble into the Churn Room, casually light a cigarette and maybe even have time to smoke it before CS_2 oblivion took him and everyone else, especially Fons.

Then he thought of Jacko and Roman and Marcus, Naseem and the other blokes in the Duracol, Parvin and most of the girls in the Coning, the spinners Qasim, Vivian, Ginger, Frank his boss. How could he hurt Mr P? Or Jean and Mel? If they lost the game this weekend they'd finish the season cowed, but this other idea was in a much murkier league.

What about his mam and dad too? There wasn't anyone to replace him and they weren't likely to have another.

It was a huge factory, and was there even a chemical combination dangerous enough to blow everything up at once? All right, a lit candle was all it took to turn their den into a charred mess, but that was minuscule and made of wood. He hadn't been able to face going back. He might never go back.

Tommy focus, a name!

He carried the latest winding to the window to see it under a different light. The shade was definitely a gold, and the special pigment had made it that way... *laal, laal, laal, laal*, it might sound like a lullaby if you sang it softly enough and there was someone to listen, someone there ready to be soothed.

Maureen Copton crowded into Tommy's mind and he let his thoughts wander.

Frank Postlethwaite swept past Victor's bench and the colourist asked, 'What's up, Frank?'

The manager walked on to where Tommy was sitting.

'Something's amusing you lad, and from the look on your face I'm not sure it's your work.'

Tommy dropped the shade card on the floor and Frank picked it up. 'My advice? Same as always - immerse yourself in the question, the answer'll come. It's only a name after all.'

With Mr P there to guide him everything had seemed possible.

'Anyway Tommy, good news. Mayor's over the moon with that last shade we sent. It wasn't the easiest job, was it, saying something about the town's past and hopes for its future. Well, I might be embellishing our contribution a bit, but we got there.'

So Tommy should be pleased. Except it wasn't a good enough reason to carry on living, was it. 'I'm grateful to you, Mr Postlethwaite, for giving me the chance.' Maureen came in to Tommy's mind again, then coincidence or what, her face appeared at the Lab door.

'I was passing, Frank. Boss wants a word.'

'Thanks Maureen, most kind.' Frank touched Tommy's arm. 'Well done.'

That left Victor and him alone.

Tommy tried to be cheerful for Frank's sake, but he soon fell back on a familiar device, and drew an invisible map, this time of how the auditorium had looked on the night of the show. He would search for clues from a time when Sunehri Saleem still occupied the same part of the world as him.

At first Tommy couldn't get beyond Pieter putting finishing touches to the summerhouse where Tommy and his lover would kiss, then Algurda Radvila wiring the tulip-shaped lamps like the ones near his Aunty Lily's in Connemara. Clive Baptiste had told him that getting involved was a chance to express himself, and he'd cornflower-blued the skies and left perfect spaces for cotton wool clouds.

On the night there must have been twenty rows of seats stretching from the temporary stage back to the serving counter. And there was Tommy, peering through the hole in the curtain before the start, with a perfect view of row five where Sunehri had just sat down next to her family.

Tommy couldn't recall anything significant in the first part, so he fast-forwarded to the interval. Again, nothing.

Reaching the second part, on the cusp of kissing his leading lady, a shiver ran through him. He'd pushed it, hadn't he! Gone further than usual. To make Sunehri jealous? Make her want him more? Doris had pushed it too, pressed her thigh against his. So it wasn't all his fault.

Recalling Sunehri's expression, she was smiling. Wasn't she? Her Uncle Naseem looked less comfortable sitting next to Nellie Bradshaw, who'd be daubed in *parfoom* pretending she'd come over from Paris specially. But he looked all right. Tommy remembered Nellie explaining that *They couldn't get mi fringe reet o'er thur, in Français*. Whereas Joan the Hairdresser's in Walton-le-Dale could? He'd enjoyed the joke. He liked the way Nellie always kept a straight face. He liked Naseem, but maybe he just didn't get it.

His mam and dad? They looked more than fine. His grandma was ill so her seat was empty. Mrs Saleem and Parvin and Tahira, well it was Tahira's last night but the lad sounded decent and they'd written a few times, exchanged photos. What Tommy had been blissfully unaware of was that it was Sunehri's last night too. Maybe she didn't even know!

She'd secretly signalled goodbye to him at the car park. *See you again tomorrow*. Wasn't that how she'd moved her lips, to form those words?

Alfonso Giorgio... maybe he had something to do with it. Why hadn't he thought of that? Yet how could it be true? She'd have told him, been upset, unless *she'd* wanted it!

Had something terrible happened?

Sunehri disappeared because something had happened to her? The police would have been round, interviewing everyone, people who worked with her, chatted in passing to her (Tommy

O'Reilly), looked at her (Tommy O'Reilly), looked for her (Tommy O'Reilly), dreamed about her (Tommy, Tommy, Tommy, Tommy). No one had been round asking any questions of any kind. That was the problem.

Right now, he'd like to sit under that plyboard tree made with such care that its leaves might shimmer on a real summer breeze. *Mosam garam*, a time for love, always time for that. Well, the tree wasn't in the canteen any longer. It would be either broken up or saved in the props cupboard by now, for a future production.

Victor could have said something about the special shade being accepted though, couldn't he? Tommy watched the Spectre enter the darkroom, then fell to gazing out of the window. A perfect day, and *Happy Cavalcade* had been the perfect artifice, and if he didn't get on with his work he'd get the perfect sack. But the weather, look at it... sunbathing, swimming in the sea if it was half warm enough, footie training, meeting a girl down Avenham.

What girl? That was never true of Sunehri anyway.

Before, it had taken fifteen minutes of fast walking from one end of the factory to the other, from Tommy O'Reilly to Sunehri Saleem.

Now that distance felt too difficult to navigate, the distance he'd need to travel from desolation back to happiness.

Tommy picked up the nearest object and smashed it down on the bench. He was horrified to see that it was Frank's expensive slide rule. Not the Aristo!

21

That Bet

'Eh, lighten up Tommy boy,' Melville said when he came in followed closely by Jean.

Tommy ignored him.

Jean began pouring water into the large glass beaker. 'Anyone for a brew?'

'I'm parched,' Melville said. 'Thanks.'

'Good timing,' said Victor. The Spectre was looking far too cheerful for Tommy's liking.

Jean placed the beaker on the tripod over the Bunsen then measured a heaped teaspoon of leaves into three smaller beakers. She checked the sugar tin. 'We've run out. I'll go and borrow some from the Test Room.'

Tommy watched the pleats of her dress catch the air like the tail feathers of the ducks on Moor Park. The first time he and Sunehri had met outside work was by chance, a Saturday afternoon. They'd circled the pond too many times to count, neither of them wanting to go home, feeling unsure of what to do instead. At one point their hands had touched. It wasn't a mistake that her hand had lingered.

Victor got everyone's attention. 'Seen this new green shade? Putting Green is what I'm calling it. The details are already recorded in the book, my last entry of many. Tommy, you are welcome to write your first shade name in, when you're ready of course.' Victor positioned some samples the colour of fresh grass in the light cabinet. 'Did Frank mention the big order coming in for my new shade, from Australia?' There was no response, and Victor continued, 'It's probably a team of golfers.'

Was that a joke? Victor didn't crack jokes.

Melville stretched and stood up. 'Passed me by. And I need the Gents.'

'Thanks for sharing that.' The Spectre sounded deflated.

Tommy forced himself to check the slide rule, to see if the alignment of the three intersecting panels was still correct. He knew from overheard conversations that even hairs-width cracks might make it snag, and if the strips weren't aligned the calculations would be out.

With the field clear, Victor jibed, 'Look at the apprentice now, struggling with a basic calculation. A bit trickier than school is it, Tommy Red?'

It was true that Tommy's knowledge of slide rules was limited to working out the amount of pigment needed for the blends, but...

Victor shook the cabinet slightly. 'Daylight lamp's going. The flickering's giving me a mild ache at the back of my eye sockets, to be truthful.'

What had that got to do with Tommy? He wouldn't be phoning the electrician for him!

'Never understood why Frank's so keen on the apprentices. Not a day's work that's useful to anyone outside themselves.'

Tommy couldn't afford to replace the sleek Aristo, especially now that he needed a new set of work clothes. Finding nothing, he went through the routine again, this time more meticulously.

'Who knows when that lamp will be replaced?' Victor said, as he went to wash some yarn samples in the sink before bleaching them.

Tommy had been in enough fights to know about walking away. Ever since that scrap behind the Pulp Store he and Fons had successfully avoided each other. It was surprising how successful they'd been, actually. He was finding it harder not to thump Victor - a lot. He thought about a recent encounter with Parvin at the main gate. *Why hadn't he asked her about Sunehri? If not then, why not walk over to the Coning right now? Could it be so difficult to do that and to say the words?*

Why not? Because Parvin'd know all right, know Tommy was keen on her cousin.

Or, he could ask Harry how he was, *Kya haal hay?*

And even if Harry didn't give much away Tommy could still read the response and know more than he did now.

Harry might come back with, *App kawn hain?*

Not, *Who are you?* But, *Who do you think you are, asking about my niece?* And, *Mr O 'Reilly, now I know everything I need to know about you, yes!*

Tommy had a sense of what most people thought about colour, that mixing it through conversation, little chats here and there along the corridor and in the canteens, walking to the bus stop after work, going to the annual dance - all that was fine as long as it stayed surface deep. It was all right to work side-by-side on the decorations for the children's party and set up the Popeye cartoons for the children and do the present-wrapping for Father Christmas. But a full-blown relationship? There was a code you couldn't transgress.

In some people's eyes mixed marriages meant mixed-up babies and whole families ruined. Idzi's views on the subject were well-known. Victor's were hidden, and Tommy suspected they weren't very broad. Then again, when he'd first met Sunehri, he had to admit to seeing the difference at first, seeing someone who wasn't like him. That was a good thing. And anyway she was probably thinking exactly the same.

He'd never understood why most people considered mixed couples *less than* rather than *more than*. He knew of a family close to home, the police always coming round, stuff nicked, a few cars burnt out, the finger pointed at them and their extended families, screaming adults, screaming babies. There were plenty of stolen goods of any description if you looked hard enough on a Saturday night after closing time. Mostly, the crime he knew about was connected to people with white faces.

'Don't say we've run out of the hydrochloric now!'

Tommy ignored Victor and found comfort in travelling along the old routes… his first few months at Atherton's loading the truck with carboys of acid, glassware, chemicals, keeping the cupboards well-stocked, keeping on the move.

'Apprentices!'

Tommy was on the verge of punching the colourist when Jean arrived with the sugar.

'Anyone else for a brew?' she asked. 'Sorry Victor, did you say something?'

'I've changed my mind.'

'Tommy, thirsty?'

'No.'

Jean tipped the leaves from the third drinking beaker back into the tea caddy.

Melville came in humming loudly.

'I'm assuming you're still parched?' Jean asked him.

'Indeed.'

Tommy gazed out of the window and wondered who he'd be with in twenty years. Forty years? Not Sunehri at this rate. They weren't even together now. They might both be dead. In 2032 the world was going to be ruled by Martians anyway. The humming began to get on Tommy's nerves and he gave Melville a sharp look. He was turning into a person who measured their lives in Guilds. It wasn't a good sign.

'Apologies. Disturbing your reveries am I?'

Maaf kar do mujhay, Tommy thought. 'Sorry Mel, I didn't mean anything.'

'Eh, no worries.'

Jean came across. Her skin smelt warm. The fine hairs on her arms made him...

'Tommy, I get the sense you're trying to communicate with me through the airwaves. Want a brew after all?'

'I give in, Jean.' Tommy watched her light the flame under the Bunsen and restart the process. It was the first time it had occurred to him how strange it was that they didn't use a kettle.

'You look banjaxed Tommy.'

'I'm not being funny Mel, but blimey - stop pestering me.'

'Can't be that bad?'

'You don't want to know.'

'And I do. Heart-ache it is, I bet.'

It dawned on Tommy that Mr P would be party to all kinds of communications as a senior member of staff. *Maybe he'd heard something important?*

'Here, dreamboat.' Jean placed a digestive biscuit next to Tommy's drink.

The beaker was too hot to pick up because it didn't have a handle. Tommy was suddenly desperate for a drink and he wondered why they didn't use mugs in the Lab either.

'Hey lad, told the team about your shade being approved?'

Mr P's enquiry came from a long way off. Tommy banged his knees on the underside of the bench.

'Well done, Tommy. First Aid box required?' Melville asked.

'Brilliant news,' Jean said.

Melville addressed Victor. 'Did you know?'

The colourist mumbled something.

Tommy felt desolate. He wanted to get out of this room. Where could he go, legitimately? Only places he'd see people he didn't want to see. His map was like a beautifully rendered, out-of-date globe that boasted the extent of the British Empire.

His manager's voice broke through. 'Want to talk to me about anything?'

'No thanks, Mr Postlethwaite.'

'Sure?'

'I'm on to it, I promise.'

Frank looked at the clock. 'Right, I'll be in my office before that meeting with Mr Atherton, if anyone wants me.'

Tommy's thoughts turned to William Atherton, the boss's great, great, ten greats grandson. One quiet afternoon Mr P had told them that, as the thirteenth of thirteen children vying for his parents' attention, William had developed a waterproof dye that when it rained didn't run down the faces of people wearing his new line of wigs. At twenty-five Atherton had built up enough capital to start a silk business in Essex, and the family had moved north. Moving, flitting. *See you again tomorrow.*

Tommy slipped a small winding of the final shade into a plastic bag. 'Going for a cigarette,' he said, standing up so fast he collided with the light cabinet. On his way to the door he looked at it hanging precariously over the edge.

'Oi!' said Melville, who managed to grab the box in time.

'Like a ballistic firework that one,' Victor cursed.

'He'll have a bruise,' said Jean. 'I suppose that's what you need in a goalie.'

'A bruise?' Victor said. 'Or do you mean a temper?'

'*Speed* is what I meant.'

Melville smiled. 'He makes some foolish mistakes, though. I'm pondering still whether to put a bet on the team winning the final game of the summer season or,' he coughed, 'losing. Any thoughts either way? Victor?'

Everyone who knew Victor Hesketh knew that he considered betting immoral.

Jean stepped in. 'I haven't heard you say thanks to Mel.'

Victor looked up. 'What for?'

'He's just saved your neons!'

The colourist frowned.

'Jean, how rude,' Melville said. 'And I can see plain enough, Victor, that you're contemplating a comfy armchair, slippers, supper... maybe cheese on toast with a neat bundle of cress on the side? A bit of telly.'

Victor concentrated on the light box. 'The natural and daylights are in place, the ultraviolet's dislodged. Juniors! Why Frank has such a soft spot I've no idea. None of his own, I suppose.'

Melville laughed. 'Yeah, and that doesn't make a difference in your case, does it.'

'Couldn't even be bothered to call an electrician.'

'Eh Victor, why not sign up for the table tennis or cricket or something? Loosen you up a bit. Crown Bowling it is tomorrow night. You don't mind Rob do you?'

'I've re-started archery,' Jean said. 'Picked up a trophy last year - I was quite pleased. Fancy archery?'

Victor tapped the side of the light box.

Melville frowned. 'See, if Tommy displays that much emotion against Ribble Motors, well, it's make or break for league position.' After rinsing a dozen bottles he set them higgledy-piggledy on the drainer. 'Stranger things have happened in the beautiful game of course.'

Victor noticed the bottles. 'That slapdash approach won't do you any favours.'

Melville pouted. 'Ooh, someone needs a holiday.'

'Wonder where Tommy's gone,' Jean said, 'left his cigarettes. It's good news about the shade.'

Melville cautiously sipped his tea from the beaker. 'You wouldn't think it, the way he's acting. So Jean, any thoughts either way? That bet?'

Jean smiled. 'No more distractions. I've work to do.'

22

Tick!

Going for a cigarette? He'd forgotten them hadn't he. And his lighter. He wouldn't be going back. His elbow ached from bashing into the light cabinet - another bruise to add to the growing display.

Tommy found himself climbing the steps to the gatehouse trying to think of the word for *cigarette* in Urdu.

How could he have forgotten it was the same?

Nicolas stood up. 'Watcha, Tom.'

'Watcha what?'

'Watcha doing here at this time of day?'

Tommy laughed. 'We should try for at spot at the Central Pier.' He secured Nicolas's seat, placed his shoes on the counter and pushed off, making the office chair spin violently. 'I'm doing nothing here, since you ask.'

'You just missed Fonsy.'

Tommy stopped the spin. 'What did he want?'

'Nothing, like you.'

On the neat shelf behind Nicolas's head - Mr Embley was an ex-service man - Tommy spotted his torch. The end was blackened but it looked all right otherwise. It was expensive, a nineteenth birthday gift from his mam and dad, bought from the ironmonger's in Fishergate. Less than a year later and it looked like he was donating it to Atherton's. He mustn't, just mustn't, say anything that would connect him to the burnt-out den, though he sensed that Nicolas already knew. His one option was to grab the torch when Mr Embley wasn't looking. Nicolas was too quick. Tommy clicked the fountain pen lid on and off, on and off. 'Say anything did he, our Alfonso Giorgio?'

A horn honked and Nicolas went to the window. 'Got a stomach ache, he said.'

'Mention my name?'

'No.' Nicolas winked, then turned to grab a delivery note dangling from a lorry driver's hand.

Tommy went off in the right direction for work, changed his mind, and dipped inside the poky toilets on the ground floor. He knew he could get away with smoking here, or since he lacked cigarettes, be alone.

Noticing that one of the cubicles was closed, its *Occupied* sign showing, Tommy waited.

The latch clicked. Fons came out.

'Stomach-ache sorted, Alfonsy?' Tommy hadn't meant to say that. It was the thought on his mind. He hadn't actually meant to say it.

'What's that to do with you?' Fons jostled into position in front of the sink where Tommy was standing, though there were two others to choose from.

Tommy grudgingly made way, then watched the prolonged hand-washing.

'Who've you been talking to?' Fons asked.

Tommy wanted his rival to disappear. *He* wasn't going to

leave first. For several long seconds they held each other's stares in an indirect way through their reflections. To Tommy this felt more like play-fighting, and he thought of that other life where he had a brother.

The toilet mirror was one of the factory's few remaining with cut edges and old-fashioned geometric patterning similar to their sherry glasses at home. The last time Tommy had been here was with Sunehri. He'd pivoted her round to see the way they looked together. *Bohut khoob*. Couldn't be better. Right.

Fons neatened his shirt collar. 'What're you doing here my friend? Pining mebbe?'

Tommy continued to hold the look. 'Dogsbody.'

'That girl Sunny. Left, didn't she.'

Tommy grabbed the top of Fons's arms and yanked him round so that they were face-to-face.

'Oi, geddoff!' Fons pulled Tommy's hands away. 'I don't want another. I need the job - don't know about you.'

'So why act like that?' Tommy thought him handsome.

Fons made an innocent face.

He *was* looking for a fight! Tommy wanted to tear him apart.

After a few gaping moments Fons sniffed. 'It's another one of your tricks. You saw me come in, followed me, didn't you.'

'Don't flatter yourself, mate.'

Fons skirted round Tommy to dry his hands.

Nothing more was said until Fons was by the exit. 'She wasn't half bad though.'

Tommy sprang from his heels and reached the door as it slammed shut. When he opened it he could see the assistant striding across Viscose Alley, his purple shirt lolling like a flower, mocking him.

Tommy shouted some curses and held on to the frame to stop himself from doing worse. Was Fons just goading him, or was it true, about him and Sunehri?

He went back inside. That last time, well, Tommy still had the memory of Sunehri's lips moving to say the word, *choomna*, but no longer the knowledge of her kiss on his lips.

He ran the hot tap and drew a few droplets of tepid water through his hair, pleased to find sufficient Brilliantine to recover the sweep of his quiff. He leant forward to check his teeth - pretty good in spite of the years of penny sweets. He understood why girls went for him. He did.

Did he?

He made his reflection act out *khush* and maintain the false smile signifying *happy* until his jaws ached. He went in to a cubicle and afterwards washed his hands fastidiously.

The swatch of yarn was burning a hole in his pocket.

He brought it out to look. It was like a vibrant golden sun that gave no warmth. By now Tommy knew the shade recipe off by heart, the exact percentage of every pigment that had made it what it was. All he had to do was come up with a name. Easier than creating the shade in the first place? It didn't seem like it.

Knowing that he needed to start somewhere, Tommy started with the names on the first page of the Standard Shade Book:

Post Office Red (a good start)
Green (boring)
Black (boring)

Light Blue (boring)
Champagne *(wish fulfilment... he didn't know*
anyone who'd drunk champagne, and naming a
shade was easier than owning a bottle - should be!)
Medium Blue *(very boring)*
Gold *(fairly boring)*

He skipped through the later pages of the book, most of which he knew off by heart:
Belladonna *(Alfonso Giorgio = poison)*
Rose Pink *(he'd have called it Rose Bonbon)*
Butterscotch *(he'd like to taste some)*
Aurelia *(not golden enough)*
Skintone *(almost pure white like a corpse and*
nothing like the colour of Sunehri's skin - Spectre
Hesketh must have come up with that name)
Mouse Grey

Although the later names in the book were more imaginative than the first, Victor's joke about the new green shade was better than most of them. So what now for inspiration?

Sunehri had taught him the colours as a reward for acquiring the numbers up to twenty. The shade in his hand, was it more of an orangey-gold or maybe a yellowy-gold? A *peelaa-sunehri rang*? Yellow was an important part of the recipe. *Sunehri*, he thought, and her intensity wouldn't let him go.

If only you were here now.

"I'm precious, Tommy. That is what my name means, resplendent, golden." The bus was approaching the factory stop, going in the direction of home. "And do not forget it."

104

They had only just met.

Blazing Orange? Blazing Naraanji sounded quite good, but he'd be giving something away about his connection with her, the way she described her world. His old English teacher would have called *naraanji* onomatopoeic because it sounded like juice squirting on your tongue as you said it. Urdu names weren't likely to go down that well with the sales reps though, were they. Maybe he should try one, watch the reaction. Then again, maybe not.

Why not? Was he a coward?

He knew that Sunehri was too *khubsurat* for some people to see beyond her face and body, too beautiful to understand how kind and funny and principled and challenging she was. Tommy was under no illusions. Even Jacko had sometimes shown interest, though he'd never come out with anything specific.

Fons was the worst, always looking for an opportunity with girls. He'd probably sensed a connection between them and decided to see how far he could take it. Or maybe there was something going on? She'd never said anything about being pestered by Fons.

Maybe she'd wanted it.

God, he was being thick!

Sunehri wasn't even here for anyone to love her or reject her or fight for her.

For all he knew, there might be some Pakistani lads known to her family who were being introduced to her right this very minute. People from his background didn't hear much about that kind of thing.

Sunehri, Resplendent, Precious, Golden, Glorious. Words.

105

Who was going to care about what you called a few threads of artificial silk?

Tommy remembered the kiss, right where he was standing.

Yes, he thought, *jee haan!*

23

Whispering

Tommy's feet found the rumpled tarmac at the edge of the road. He went inside the same building again using an adjacent door, and made his way up, taking the stairs two at a time. He almost fell in to the Lab.

Victor looked across at the sound of panting. 'Tommy Red, so soon?' He raised his eyebrows at the clock.

Jean seemed relieved to see him. 'Leave off, Victor.'

Since the manager wasn't around, Victor wouldn't leave off. 'Frank's quick with the shade names, so why give the apprentice so much slack?'

Tommy's ears were bursting, never mind stuffed with cloth like Melville sometimes said. Most important of all, massively more important than trying to get up the Spectre's nose, he had the name he wanted, and for now he would only tell Mr P. Nobody would ever know who had inspired the name.

'Calling Tommy Red... tick, tick, tick!'

Tommy stayed fast. No matter what Victor Hesketh said, he knew that the success in creating the shade was down to his eye for colour, listening to Mr P's advice - always that - and the determination to make his own luck.

The oven beeped and the colourist went to see to it.

Tommy knew well enough that he'd been motivated by Sunehri's growing attachment, and with this realisation he understood something about Victor too. Being passed over for the special job when he was the more senior - that's why his feet had been permanently stuck in a cowpat.

Where was Mr P anyway? How long could someone be when you needed them?

Melville opened the Recipe Book. 'Anyone seen Frank's Aristo? I could do with eh, borrowing it.'

Tommy took the slide rule over. 'Here, Mel. It's all right!'

Melville looked puzzled. 'Oh, Frank won't mind, as long he doesn't see me.' Before beginning his calculations Melville glanced across at the office.

Tommy followed the measurements closely and the way Melville recorded the cost of the pigments and the amount of yarn that had been spun for the customer. He'd got away with it! Mr P's slide rule was in perfect working order.

Melville licked his lips. 'I'm feeling so ravenous my vision's distorting. See here Tommy, there's a recipe for Sunday dinner, as if I needed instructions I've cooked them often enough - my job as a boy, chef to the whole family. Look, roast potatoes, a leg of lamb, peas and a few fingers of carrot.'

Tommy thought of his dad doing the pots after a Saturday fry-up and he wondered... could he talk to him about Sunehri? He dug his fingernails into his palms to kill the idea, then wondered what kind of animal would make a bite like that.

When Mr P arrived Tommy went straight over to him, 'Guild Glory Gold,' he said quietly.

'What's that when it's at home?' the manager asked.

Tommy whispered, 'The special shade?' He sensed that Victor was hovering. 'Mr Postlethwaite, it's all right to close your door isn't it?'

The manager nodded, looking concerned. 'What is it?'

'The name for the new shade.'

'I see,' Mr Postlethwaite whispered. 'Sorry, I'm being a bit slow. Got a lot on my mind. Why the whispering?'

'The Town Hall, they don't need to approve the name as well as the colour Mr P, do they? And Mr P, you can speak normally now - the door's shut.'

Frank laughed. 'I told the Committee we'd send a few ideas, maybe it's for a news story, I don't know. This name you've come up with, I quite like it. All I'd say is, it's a bit long. We don't generally use three-word names.'

Tommy was minded to tell Mr P about the very first shade in the book and a couple more recently. He decided against it. 'See, what I was thinking Mr P was, after, we can just call it Glory Gold, for the regular orders.'

Saying these words made Tommy think of her more. Surely the whole world must know that he loved Sunehri Saleem and that his heart was broken? The story that gnawed away at him was about a White boy from Preston who had no right to ask questions and less of a right to receive answers.

So what was left? A few threads of artificial silk.

He might never hear from her again.

Tommy pulled his gaze from the sample of golden yarn. *Sunehri*, it said. Even as he looked away, more loudly it said her name to his eyes and his flesh and everything that was Tommy O'Reilly.

24

Tea at the O'Reilly's

Tommy stayed late at work by mistake, then took the longest route home. He pushed his bike into the ginnel down the side and used the back entrance, hoping he wouldn't have to speak to anyone.

'In here.' It was his mam calling from the front room. Tommy went in and noticed three things out of place:

1. The room was spotless.
2. His mam and his dad were sitting round the big table mid-week.
3. A young woman about his age was with them.

Tommy smiled at her. 'Who are you?'

'Hello,' she said.

'I've seen you before.' Tommy thought that her clothes were more suited to a Sunday Service.

'Carol works in the pet shop, in Lucas Street,' his dad explained.

'In town?'

Carol nodded. 'Where do you work, Tommy?'

'Atherton's.'

'How long've you been there?' she asked.

'How long have you been *there?*' he asked.

'Worked at H Farrington?'

'Is that the big pet shop in town?'

Carol nodded. 'I was sixteen when I started. I help out at my aunty and uncle's shop a bit too.'

'Thought I'd seen you somewhere,' he said.

Annie O'Reilly blustered into the kitchen and Tommy cornered her. 'What's going on, mam?'

She shushed her son and finished placing the floral china on the tray.

Tommy ran up to his room and dragged the heftiest book from the stack, then raced down again and slammed the volume so hard on the table that the ornaments in the front room rattled. He crossed his legs and began to read.

At first Tommy enjoyed the feeling of everyone's eyes on him and the silence he'd enforced by his own silence. He took mental bets on who would speak first, tell him he was a rude sort, tell him to stop. When no one did, he began saying the words aloud:

> *Fifty fighters, two chiefs at the head*
> *One was Hunter, son of Bloodlust...*

Tommy was surprised when it was Carol who asked, 'What're you reading?'

'By this point in the book - Carol, is it? - many thousands of warriors have been slaughtered and we're only at...' he looked for the page number in *The Iliad*, 'see, we've barely got going and it's already rivers of *laal*.' Tommy blushed to hear himself using Sunehri's language in company, and he wouldn't have escaped a director's note from Maureen for that delivery.

To kill the embarrassment, he decided to layer on another slice of ham:

Son of Bloodlust,
Strong as the Gods, son of Killerman,
Cut-throat Slaughter...

Annie looked at her husband. 'He doesn't have to say it so loud, does he? We're only in the house!' She smiled at Carol. 'He's partial to the acting, our Tommy.' Trying to draw the visitor's eye to the latest show programme on the mantelpiece, Annie O'Reilly asked, 'Did yer see...?'

Tommy spoke over his mam's words, 'Homer. Heard of him, Carol?' and he continued reading out loud:

To think these hundred troops do march
With voices held in chests and so much silence...

His mam reached for the milk jug and knocked it over. She saw to the spill straight away, dousing it with the pot towel that had been draped over her shoulder. The visitor tried to grab the towel as the milk ran towards the lip of the table, but Annie held on and said she wasn't to fuss.

The liquid cascaded over the edge and they watched the droplets spread into stains on Carol's dress.

Tommy shut his book with a bang. 'Look at the state of you Mam - stop it!' He noticed his dad's face and was sorry about that, but not about anything else.

When the flurry was over Tommy watched the visitor take a bite from her slice of bread. The islands of butter revealed his mam's hand. Carol Cuff's teacup stayed un-lifted.

Because he couldn't think of anything better to do, Tommy continued reading, but sensed that even he would be taking it too far if he turned the page, since he was stuck on the same words, *With voices held in chests and so much silence...*

To universal relief, a short while later the visitor stood up and smiled limply at Mr and Mrs O'Reilly.

Annie saw her out.

'Bye,' Tommy called sarcastically.

Annie cursed, but it was against herself. 'Left mi pinny on right through, didn't I.'

'Who cares?'

'Tommy, I get the place spick and spam and that's the...'

'It's *span*, not Spam.'

'I never did favour that newfangled invention. Any road, corned beef, chips, peas is what we're having fer us proper tea.'

This was the last time Carol came to the house.

After tea, Jamelia knocked and said from the pavement that she'd a new idea and the best place to discuss it was at the shop because there was someone there right now who wanted to put in her two pennyworth.

Annie found her bag and told Tommy she was going for a fresh pint of milk and some butter. To annoy her, Tommy asked if she wanted company.

'I'm off on missen, rude soul.'

On the way, Jamelia refused to be drawn about her own business. 'How'd it go in there, dear?'

'I suppose I'll be apologising to Mrs Cuff on Tommy's behalf,' Annie said. 'I'll not be walking twice the distance to that other shop. I've enough on my plate.'

The shop bell dinged. Jamelia and Annie said hello to Mrs Cuff, Carol's aunty, and Annie peered over the counter to the stock room behind. 'Is she in, your Carol?'

'It's not too busy at this time so I'm coping on my own,' Mrs Cuff said. 'Bert's out on the campaign trail, same as.' The shop's owner lowered her voice, 'We've had a few bits of what they're calling hate mail. See it on the news? Wish he'd stop raising their heckles. End it dead'd be to my liking. Nothing much wrong with them immigrants s'far my perspective's concerned. What do I know? Our Carol come over did she? Said she might call in on the way but I've not seen her.'

Annie heard a sound at the far end of the shop. She saw a woman standing with a bag of groceries by her feet. It was Parvin's mother, Falak Butt. She and Annie were acquainted through Jamelia, who knew everyone.

They looked at each other shyly from a distance until Jamelia ordered them to get on with it while she ticked the things off her shopping list - including popping into the Off Licence for a bottle of rum.

'Tell yer about yer niece another time,' Annie said to Mrs Cuff, before making her cautious way down the shop's aisle.

Annie and Falak got to talking about Atherton's, and Naseem's job in the Duracol, and the difficulties Harry had practising the piano in the terrace a few houses down with walls like paper, and how Tahira and her husband were hoping to buy a small house close to her husband's family south of Mirpur.

Eventually they got on to the subject of Falak's niece, Sunehri Saleem.

25

Arrival of the Queen of Deepdale

Next morning Tommy arrived at work without noticing the places and people he passed, and he forgot to wave at Nicolas in the gatehouse.

Friday afternoon was when everyone polished the bench-tops. Tommy volunteered to do all ten of them, which raised a few jokes. The more he cleaned, the more he noticed the ages-old chemical stains, especially on the handles, that most likely would never be removed while the factory stood.

When he got home, Tommy slunk upstairs without saying a word. He didn't even feel like reading. He stared at the cracked ceiling above his bed thinking about his mam and dad's attempt – well, mainly his mam's - to prise out a commitment from him to come on holiday.

It's only for a week.

He'd enjoy the break.

He'd been reet moody recently.

It'd do him good. Etcetera, etcetera, waghaira, waghaira.

'Since yer up, might as well pack,' his mam called to him.

Tommy's reaction was to wedge the books behind his bedroom door so that the edges butted up. How could he go off for a week when Sunehri might arrive any day? If she came home struggling with her bags - there was a route from town past their window - he could help her, couldn't he. And there was that convenient clash with the football match on Saturday, as well as the small matter of him being an adult. By his mam's comment earlier, she still hadn't accepted he wasn't going.

There was a loud knock.

Tommy went to the window. It was Jamelia again, the person closest to Ayesha, who knew the Manzoors and Butts pretty well too. *Did she know where Sunehri was?*

'I'll get it,' his mam called.

'Hello, Annie dear. All right?'

'Fine, Jamelia. What's up?'

Tommy crept downstairs. Jamelia and his mam were talking loudly as usual, so he had no trouble hearing.

'I brung you a few bits and bobs. It's not the time to go fussing over the cooking is it, night before you go away.' Jamelia was aware that Annie never did fuss over the cooking.

'Come in, Jamelia love. That's kind. Frank isn't back yet.'

Annie took the parcel wrapped in pages from the *Lancashire Evening Post,* and the visitor was directed to the kitchen table. 'Cuppa? Or I think there's a bit of sherry left. Have a sherry? I know it's for special occasions but, well, I fancy one.' Annie looked at Jamelia. 'That long pause means a *yes.*' She carried two cut glasses from the sideboard in the front room then went back for the sherry bottle.

'This is a lovely cloth, Annie. New is it?'

'Got it from my sister Lily. Chucking it out she was, and I sez, I'll have it, and here it is.' Annie put the sherry bottle down to feel the quality of the linen again. She nodded. 'Nice weight.'

Jamelia pursed her lips. 'My own cloths're getting a bit shabby, when I see this, dear.'

'I've always liked a nice tablecloth.' Annie poured them both a small, sweet sherry. 'Can't think I've used these glasses on a day that wasn't calling itself a Sunday or a Christmas.'

Jamelia wiggled to get comfortable on the hard chair and spotted the show programme under Annie's elbow. 'We've talked so much about that *other thing*, I haven't asked yer about the drama evening. So, how was it, dear? I bet he did grand, Tommy? Great shame it was I wasn't able to come. Needs a bit more attention recent like, her arthritis.'

Annie nodded. 'Sorry to hear that, Jamelia. She isn't doing any better then, yer mam?'

As Tommy sat on the bottom step with his ear to the door, memories came of sitting there as a boy, told off for something, waiting impatiently to be forgiven, warm molasses smelling of home and happiness seeping through the cracks in the wood, eventually being called through for a round of buttery treacle on toast.

'Frank Postlethwaite, Frank from the factory, we came home in his car,' Annie said. 'It were a reet smooth ride. *Our* Frank said so.'

'I don't want to hear about coming home already, dear.'

'Oh, that boss a' Tommy's!'

Jamelia nodded. 'Falling on his feet like that.'

Both women took a genteel sip of sherry.

'We had a reet good time, Jamelia.'

Tommy wished his mam and dad would sometimes go beyond saying they'd had *a reet good time* when they returned from Bingo, The Acregate, an occasional trip to Blackpool. Why couldn't they say they *hadn't* enjoyed something for a change, or not enjoyed this as much as that, and was it really too much to expect the occasional reason why?

'Front row seats we had. Tommy reserved them down from the VIPs and I asked Frank about that, Tommy's Frank from work. VIPs means Very Important People, Jamelia. And those counsellors in all their posh suits, they did some polite clapping and the Mayor, he sez summat about these special flags or summat that Atherton's is doing and how he'll be cutting the ribbon on that new Guild Hall as soon as it's ready.'

'I'll be going to that, on Lancaster Road. I don't know there's a date yet.'

'Oh, and t'Mayoress with her dark blue suit...'

'Listen Annie dear, we'll be here all night if I only hear about what people was wearing. In fine voice Tommy, was he?'

Annie laughed and took another sip of sherry. 'Oh, was he. Reet good.'

Tommy nearly swore out loud at his mam's laziness.

'Voice like velvet, Jamelia, and his acting! We felt that proud. And Jean, that girl in Tommy's laboratory, she's a beautiful voice. And Harry, you mun tell him when yer seen him, moving from one tune t'tother as fast as... Oh, you know what they had?'

Jamelia shook her head.

'A speedcar. Tommy were run o'er wi' it!'

At first Jamelia laughed, then she stopped. 'That's terrible, dear. Run over?'

'Well, yer didn't actually *see* the car. There were these

screeches and screams and the like and Harry's playing the keys right at t'bottom o' pianer. Then it was *My Old Man*. Belted it out, I did. *And don't dilly dally on the waaaay*! Dad joined in a bit, most likely mouthing the words, silly man, but he were happy enough.'

'So dear, he enjoyed himself Frank, did he?'

Annie's sherry glass was almost empty. 'And they did *Marezee dotes and dozy dotes...* Oh, listen to me tripping over. It got to everyone's tongues and we did have a good laugh.'

Jamelia shifted in her chair. 'Aw, I wished I'd have not missed it. Next time fer definite.'

Annie returned the sherry bottle to the sideboard and Jamelia stood up to go. 'When we catched up with Tommy he were being clapped on t'back by first aiders, voluntary like, probably relieved it were nothing more than sore throats from all that cheering and singing. No drunks, neither. Tea and biscuits is all they put on.' Annie gave the programme to Jamelia.

'Oh, that's a strong design, with Tommy's name all big. That lad, honestly... and Doris Smith. Keen on Doris, is he?'

Annie shook her head. 'Not really, no. I don't really think so. How's Ayesha Saleem getting on? Mrs Butt didn't have that much to say.'

Tommy's heart started to pound so hard that, with the additional barrier between them, he feared he might miss what he'd been longing to find out.

'The Saleems have just arrived,' Jamelia said.

'Must be hot, over there in Pakistani.'

'I hear there's lots to do still, Annie. Weddings is demanding. Always was, always will be. Amen.'

Whose wedding?

Was she talking about Tahira's wedding?

Or someone else's entirely?

26

Curry and Rice and HP Sauce

Annie inspected Jamelia's package. 'So what've you brung us?'

'Chicken and rice, quite spicy. I put a green chilli in so mek sure you've a glass of milk nearby. Ever tried coconut milk?'

Annie opened the newspaper. 'Mmmm, smells good. Is it fer were tea? Frank won't like it, though Tommy's quite keen on the spices.'

'It's up to you, dear. It'll save. I just thought, both working all week and off on holiday in the morning.'

'That's kind.'

'Well, you gave us that gooseberry pie last week - from the bakery.' Jamelia stood up. 'I'll be there next time fer definite. Christmas, is it? I'll fetch she, knees or no knees.'

Annie laughed. 'Yer mam might not feel like it if she's not got no knees!'

'She might join in with singing *Knees Up, Mother Brown,* if they're planning on doing that old timer.'

'We'll see what Frank's in the mood fer. Tommy's in, so I'll ask him.'

Jamelia lowered the volume. 'Oh, Tommy's home is he? *He's* keeping quiet.' The women's voices were swallowed by the vestibule and Tommy was left stranded.

When Frank O'Reilly arrived home, the first thing he did was wash off the foundry dirt and change into clean clothes.

Annie brought the food and they ate in silence.

When three sets of knives and forks were laid side-by-side on three empty plates Tommy's mam said, 'That's it fer me. If yer can't be civil then it's as well yer not coming.'

How was being silent not civil? He hated it here.

'Well, if no one's saying nowt, I'm off up to sort missen. Tommy can wash up.'

Frank's voice was warm, trying to make the peace as usual, 'Annie, I'll do it.'

'If yer like,' she said.

Frank strode to the sink on his lanky legs. 'Fetch things please, Tom.'

Sunehri's dark eyes speckled with green, that's what Tommy was looking at, not the plates smeared with leftover HP sauce and warmed up chicken curry, or the rice grains left in the pan or the yellow smear of his dad's kippers or the dregs of tea or the crumbs that added their off-white patterning to the embroidered tablecloth. Her voice filled his mind, as inventive as the blackbird that sang from their yard wall when the sun was setting, not the gentle sound of his dad asking him to help.

'Fetch things over,' his dad repeated.

As Tommy stood up it felt as though his brains had fallen to mush. Jamelia had just said that the Saleems had arrived in Pakistan, or *Pakistani* as his mam always referred to it. Since Mr Saleem was usually there anyway working, it must be Sunehri who had gone with her maa.

So that was it.

122

No more sights or sounds of her, no scent of her.

Tommy cleared the table, did the wiping, put the pots and cutlery away.

If she was there, well, it was thousands of miles from Preston, from his house, this street.

He hadn't even made it to Manchester yet.

Pakistan was completely hopeless.

At least she was safe.

Safely away from him?

Frank O'Reilly didn't ask why Tommy wasn't shaking out the tablecloth or sweeping the kitchen flags, or why he was going at half-pace on the things he was doing. 'You'll do, Tom. Go and get packed. Coming, aren't yer? Mam'll be disappointed if tha's not.'

He hated letting his dad down. But he'd decided. Not even for a week, not for any time and not for any reason that might come up from now until the last second of leaving. 'It's the final tomorrow, Dad.' Tommy shifted awkwardly. 'I haven't booked the time off work.'

'You didn't tell us about that Tom, about yer work.' Frank weighed the options. 'I'll talk her round. One thing, it's only a small thing, mind.'

Tommy had no idea what his dad was going to say.

'Replace that privy glass you broke I don't know when. You've seven days to do it, well five-and-a-bit not counting match day and the morning after.'

Tommy smiled. 'Right, Dad.'

'That putty'd better be skinned over, time we're back.'

Frank went to sit in his comfy chair. He opened the paper to check the next day's racing tips. 'Another thing - cheer up.'

Annie kept herself to herself upstairs. This was unusual and it set Tommy and Frank on edge.

Once the horses had been chosen, Frank riffled through the thin contents of the magazine rack. Finding nothing of interest he went to the kitchen for the sheets of newspaper Jamelia had used for wrapping the box of curry.

'Tom, look!'

'What?'

'You and the gang, Atherton's Drama Club.'

Tommy looked over his dad's shoulder and saw the write-up of *Happy Cavalcade*. There was one photo, and it was of him and Doris kissing. 'Maureen said she'd invited the paper, put a ticket by. I never saw anyone.'

'Mam'll be pleased.'

'Maybe.'

The clock sounded nine as Frank placed his large hand on the latch. 'Right, I'll be off up to pack. Early to rise.'

'Night, Dad.'

Tommy lay on his bed fully-clothed and woke up a few hours later feeling uncomfortable. His mouth was rancid, he'd not brushed his teeth and he needed a piss. Once in bed again, his mam started snoring and his dad coughing. Tommy listened.

As he was making his morning brew, a waft of perfume rolled into the kitchen like a red mist. Tommy hated perfume, always had. He wondered if last night's argument had prompted his mam to lather it on. Enough smells assaulted him at work.

More odours were added when his dad made the Saturday

fry-up. Tommy was looking forward to having the place to himself. He'd learnt how to ignore the CS2 at work and he didn't mind the soapy cakewash, or even the chlorine - which was like going to the baths - but for some reason the bacon smell was really irritating him this morning. A week away and everyone had to feel less mithered than this. He could bake them a cake. He might even wash it first. *Don't be stupid, Tommy!*

His mam swept past in a flowery pinny, the thick straps just about containing her bosom. 'Noel'll be here soon enough,' she said in a flat voice.

In the half-hour before Tommy's cousin arrived his mam decided to tidy the ornaments, even though she'd done it for Carol Cuff's visit. A weather gauge with the legend "A Present From Blackpool" was lifted up and dusted. Then it was the turn of the Fanny Freckleface doll, a tombola prize from the Club. First the doll was wiped with spit then rubbed with the pocket of her pinny. Tommy was curious to know why the doll always had special treatment, and realised it was not the perfect time to ask. A crude bamboo wheel on the shelf below was a birthday present from the weaving ladies and his mam always gave it a spin on its wobbly axis. Today she bent her knees so that her mouth was level with the mantelpiece, and blew hard enough to send several years of Drama Society programmes across the room. One fell in the coal scuttle and gained an instant bruise.

Frank put the belted suitcase down carefully. 'I'll get it.' He dusted the sooty paper with his handkerchief and returned the display to normal. Then he folded his wife's pinny and helped her on with her summer coat.

The three stood awkwardly.

When the knocker went, everyone jumped.

'That'll be Noel,' said Tommy's dad.

Noel was holding his car door open like a chauffeur, posing. He gestured to his younger cousin. 'Coming in the front?'

'No.' Tommy followed his parents to the car. 'Bye, Mam.' They hugged lightly. That was good. 'Bye, Dad.'

Before getting behind the wheel Noel said, 'I might call round in the week, then.'

'And I might be out *then*,' Tommy muttered.

The window was slowly wound down and Annie called, 'Be good, son. Big piece in the paper, weren't it.'

Tommy smiled. He waited until the car had gone round the corner, on to Sunehri's road, then he went inside. His parents were due to hitch up with various brothers and sisters and work friends then catch the train and ferry to Ireland. He wouldn't miss them. Seven days, that was all.

He changed into his football togs and cycled to the pitch they used for home games. Jacko was already there doing ball tricks and Tommy wished he'd stayed at home, feigned an illness or something. During penalty practice they were on better form than expected, which cheered him up a bit.

'It'll come down to those little mitts of yours,' Jacko told him. 'It'll be *that* close Tommy. Do your job!'

They went to Jacko's for cheese and crackers then came back out to join the rest of the team on the pitch. Though the weather was drizzly, come three o'clock there was a fair turn-out, with a handful of supporters on each side. A couple of people walking their dogs swelled the numbers. Tommy noticed that Fons was one of the spectators standing on their side, no doubt hoping to witness a particular humiliation.

Melville arrived and waved from the line. 'Come on, the Blues!' During the match his running commentary interspersed with instructions was only briefly interrupted - when Tommy let in the two goals.

Luckily Jacko scored three.

When the ref blew the final whistle a Factory Blues supporter made his way sheepishly across the pitch and gave the striker a "well done". Tommy watched the Ribble Motors lot slinking off for a consolation pint at The Crown, and he wondered, *What next?*

Melville bounded over. 'Hero of the match, Jacko. And you didn't do too bad Tommy, all things considered.'

'Thanks Mel. What things considered?'

'You know, having us biting our finger-ends till that last sweet minute when Jacko scored his third.'

'Oh that. Well, as you haven't been keeping tally, I've saved more than I've missed this season.'

Melville patted him on the arm. 'And don't start getting dark. Yesterday I couldn't make up my mind whether to place a bet for or against. Eh, I didn't mean to tell you that. I called it right, though, so I'll treat yous both to a pint o' best.'

'That's guilt talking,' said Jacko. 'You're on.'

Tommy hadn't been to The Acregate since... he couldn't remember the last time.

'No trophy,' said Melville, 'but our prospects for the main season have instantly gone up. Did I say I was thinking of joining the team?'

'Don't be daft,' said Jacko. 'Your belly's as fat as that porker strung up in George Ramsey's window.'

'True enough. Then again you don't have my intellect.' Melville turned to leave. 'I'll be kept waiting ten minutes at the bar - that's plenty for changing your boots. Any longer and the offer's withdrawn.'

'We'll stink,' said Jacko.

'We'll be there,' said Tommy. He saw Fons hovering on the path. It seemed unlikely, but maybe he wanted to come with them. There was no chance to find out because he'd left by the time they were ready.

27

A Painting

This painting provides all perspectives. Each perspective changes according to the wishes of the viewer. I am the viewer.

Under my bed I see a couple of scummy mugs, books with bookmarks, a skewed pile of football magazines, wonky mattress springs, uneven wadding, a crumpled hankie.

On top of the bed something is laid out, a dead body I didn't notice at first. It's me. It's definitely my outline.

I feel the pull of a desire that doesn't belong to me as I watch, as I'm watched.

I can't find it, or them, inside the painting or outside it, but I sense what they want, and that their will is stronger than mine.

They want the perspective to drop.

I can't resist the pull, and anyway as a live/dead person I'm curious. I didn't ask to be in this painting and I want to know what will happen to my body if the perspective on my body changes. Maybe I'll come alive in both places - that's if I'm still alive in this one.

I allow everything to sink to the soil beneath the house. I'm still looking up, from the foundations upwards. My shape is lying there in the centre like an abandoned corpse.

Should I feel more connected to it than I do?

Looking right through my own house is probably enough to think about for now.

The floorboards are like glass, so none of the objects placed on them are lost. In some ways they're as solid and recognisable as usual, such as Dad's armchair. At the same time I'm aware that the situation is not at all ordinary.

At the gable end is the wall that's three times higher than the ends of the other terraces. Seventy-five per cent of this wall belongs to Waverley Mill where Mam works. It's hanging on with a line of checked pot towels and pinnies in the same red and white and dark blue and white pattern.

As the perspective widens beyond the house to Cuff's corner shop, Preston, Blackpool, Liverpool, Manchester, Lancashire, as it spreads to Britain, Ireland, Pakistan, India, the painter's line grows smudged.

Who is the painter?

I know it isn't me, and I also know that my shortcomings have caused the line to blur.

Whoever's fighting for control over this painting views the world so differently from me.

They could show me the world differently.

28

Arrival of the Queen of Soda Breads

With no parents to nag him Tommy could stay in bed as long as he wanted. This helped, because he had a Sunday hangover in spite of only downing a couple after the game.

His mind ran to Guild Week and the fairground that would be set up on Moor Park. He wondered if the same family would be running it as last Bank Holiday, Wilcocks was it? That bloke who'd ratcheted up the Waltzer until it didn't seem legal, tubs shooting across the circle and forcing his ribcage against the steel bar, ramming the air out of his lungs.

He lay for hours. Thankfully there was no postman today to bring no letter. Maybe she *had* written. Why didn't he even know how long it took for a letter to get here from different parts of the world, say from Pakistan?

Tommy went out to the yard in his pyjamas and puttied in a new privy window. After all that avoiding he was soon back in bed. From his pile of library books he chose *Love on the Dole* and from the library stamps inside the front cover he mentally ticked what were probably his own four loans in the past year. He turned to the page with the hand-made bookmark, Sunehri's picture of him as a satisfied worm wearing glasses, and read:

She frowned. 'Aach, what d'y'think I am? And don't say "mek", it's "make". Oh, I've no time to muck about - I mean, mend collars for nobody...'

Tommy sat up, remembering the shirt with the oil stain that he'd stuffed in the wardrobe weeks ago. He found the carbolic soap under the kitchen sink and, after quarter of an hour of applying it to the streak on the sleeve, he was satisfied. He hooked the hanger on the drying rack and hoisted it with the pulley to the kitchen ceiling. It would be dry and ironed by the time his mam and dad returned from holiday. He noticed his clean nails and longed for the time when they were stained bright red.

On Monday morning he left so late that he didn't have time for breakfast at home. He went to the men's canteen and asked the cook to make him up a bacon butty.

'Where's the bacon then, Tommy?'

'Give him the two slices of bread. He won't notice any different!' It was Fons, standing too close.

The cook laughed with Fons.

Tommy was seething. 'I suppose canteen bacon will have to do,' he said, handing over his last bit of money to the cashier. 'A distant second.'

Fons sauntered away and Tommy watched him lean over a table of girls by the entrance to the women's canteen. Michelle and Parvin from the Coning were among them, and that new girl Jenny.

Even though going to the Duracol department in the Caves was part of his job, whenever he spotted Harry or Naseem, Tommy got into the habit of calling back later to catch Jacko or

132

Idzi. He avoided going over to the Coning too.

At home he fell into the habit of not cooking so he wouldn't have to wash up. In spite of this, the place was a tip in days. Even if Jamelia came round, even though she might be the key to Sunehri Saleem, he'd already decided to confine all visitors to the front step.

Before bed, Tommy would sit in front of the triptych of mirrors, swivelling the angles for a new perspective. No matter how strange the eyes that looked out, they remained his eyes. He wanted them to be different so that he might move on.

At bedtime he'd lie there trying to see himself as others did. Dangerous? A bit of a lad? His shoes always shone though they were far from the best you could buy. His dad might be able to make the ones he had now last through another winter. 'Doing mine... son?' Never assuming anything.

And that wish for him to cheer up? The more Tommy mooched about the house the more his mood went in the opposite direction.

The night before his parents came back from holiday Tommy tossed and turned for hours.

Wasn't it more about what you wanted for your own future than fitting in with other people's versions of how the world should be?

And what was the use of not doing something because you were afraid of the consequences, when you didn't know, not really, what rules you were breaking?

Eventually Tommy got up and punished himself by pacing the cold kitchen floor. It was close to two in the morning when he left the house in his pyjamas and bare feet, took two steps, and hammered on Jamelia's front door.

No answer. He didn't expect an answer.

He didn't even look up to see if the curtain was moving.

A few minutes later Tommy lurched back to bed with stinging knuckles and a parched throat. His mind was a frizz of broken filaments. He stuffed his face into his pillow and allowed the melody of a Bobby Hebb song to play on his heartstrings, 'Sunehri, tomorrow my life will surely... get even worse.'

Moments before his parents walked in with the soda bread, Tommy had finished drying the week's-worth of dirty pans and plates and chucking the mouldy breadcrumbs out for the birds - not that they'd find them too attractive.

'Yer Aunty Eileen got up early,' his mam said. 'Have a sniff.'

'Very fresh.' Tommy felt relieved he'd left the door open.

This year's holiday ornament was a painted pot dog with a cheeky face. One of its ears was permanently clamped up, the other permanently clamped down. Tommy considered it perfect; the down ear would shut out the noise of the arguments that would soon ensue between him and his mam, and the up ear would be listening for a mood change. The weaving loom was shoved along to make space on the shelf.

'I did the window, Dad.'

'Good, Tom. How's it been?'

'All right.' Tommy saw his dad looking at his knuckles, and knew he wouldn't say anything. 'How was your holiday?'

'Reet good,' said his mam. 'Didn't manage to coincide with Lily. We missed you too.' She touched his arm. 'Kept it tidy!'

Tommy saw her looking at the wet patch in front of the sink.

At Atherton's, Tommy worked as hard as he needed to, helped out where he'd get maximum credit, and took enough cigarette breaks to finish a pack of forty in the time it took to light a candle and make a few shadow shapes and kiss her and for everything to end.

The siren went at the close of the week and Tommy tied a card label to a winding of Glory Gold and placed it in a little plastic bag. He'd keep the sample in his dressing table at home, a memento.

Once arrived at home, Tommy went upstairs and shut the winding in the marquetry-fronted drawer. He caught his reflection. He might change his image. Hairstyles were getting longer over the ears, with full-blown sideburns - more of a tousled look and not too slick. Jacko was growing his hair and he'd told Tommy yesterday that he was contemplating a bubble perm like George Ross, Jim McNab, the PNE lot. He was already a bit thin on top, so Tommy had said that the extra volume might help fill the gaps, and when it got really bad he could opt for a Charlton brush-over. Tommy wondered what the Urdu word for *bald* was. No idea, and nobody to ask.

He scrutinised his front view, side view, half view, mid positions, a tracking shot in reverse. He decided that the long sideburns could stay, but a quiff and hair down the nape of the neck - did they go together? He grabbed the comb and brushed his long fringe forward.

He burst out laughing. *No one on the planet would be interested in going out with that!* 'Spell on me, Su-u-ne-hreeee...' he sang like Pavarotti.

Tommy froze when he heard a noise downstairs.

'Is that you already, Tommy?'

'Mam?' He preferred Sunehri's word, *Maa*.

Tommy shifted the pillar of books and looked out.

Annie O'Reilly appeared at the bottom of the stairs. She waited for him to speak.

'What do you think of these new hairstyles, you know, growing it longer?'

'Like a wet rag gone frayed. Get down t'barbers and give it a good cutting is what I allus say.'

Tommy laughed. 'Right, Mam, I've heard that one before. You need to keep up with the times.'

29

Explosion

At work, just after dinnertime, Harry followed his brother Naseem into the Lab. When Tommy heard the word *Salaam* and the brothers talking in English and Urdu he realised how much he'd missed Sunehri's language. He picked up that it was doff time for half a dozen machines, that Naseem had wound a yarn sample onto a 1½ inch frame in the Spinning department, and that they had a shade query for Mr P relating to this card winding. He heard Naseem say that he'd come back later, as Mr P was out.

Melville called over. 'Fancy a brew first?'

Naseem gave a short wave. 'That is kind, no.'

'See yous around then.'

Tommy could follow them out, couldn't he, ignore Spectre Hesketh's comments about him turning into a chain smoker. He could be in that corridor in seconds talking to both of Sunehri's uncles about her and he might know everything he'd wanted to know all these weeks, even if it was a confirmation that he had lost her. He stood up to leave.

'Anyone else?' Melville's offer was cut short by a booming sound. 'Victor, let off a big one have you?'

Victor raised his eyebrows, his attention fixed on Tommy.

The factory's alarm sounded.

Mr Postlethwaite came in and addressed the team. 'Safety Officer's this minute told me a fire's broken out in the Spinning. He'll keep us updated. Don't evacuate yet. Stay here please, or very close by.'

'Right you are,' said Melville. 'Haven't seen Jean for a bit. I'm sure she'll be fine, but just to let you know, Frank.'

'Noted.'

A fire raging in the Spinning department? That qualified as being very close by. Who had Tommy seen so far? Qasim, Vivian, Tony Tubbs, and there'd be another seventy men or so on the machines for the day shift. He'd always been rubbish at sitting still.

'Frank...' Victor said, pointing out the departing Tommy.

Frank Postlethwaite said to Melville quietly, 'Is it me, or is the lad taking a lot of breaks?'

Melville gave a concerned look as Tommy tried to make his getaway.

'Where you off to, lad?'

Tommy paused by the door. 'Mr Postlethwaite, I need to ask Harry something about... a shade match.'

'What shade's that?'

Mr P was calling him on it. He'd never done that before. Tommy sensed the danger in putting his manager's back up, but the fire might be over by the time he got to the Spinning if he didn't get a move on. 'That new version of Belladonna, the purple, Mr Postlethwaite. We're taking out some of the err... it's too over-powering what we've got now.' Tommy restrained a smile. *Would he get away with it?*

138

'Who's we?'

'Well, I was going to talk to Naseem about it.'

'I thought you said Harry. Anyway, they were both in the corridor a minute ago. There and back, Tommy. You're on strict orders now and no messing.'

'Right you are, Mr Postlethwaite.'

Tommy didn't get far because cordons had been put up round the Spinning department. Eventually he managed to reach one of the windows where he could see Parwez, Qasim, Tony Tubbs, Ginger and some of the other spinners being directed out at the far end, followed by Wadi with a couple of fire stewards; it looked like he was in shock.

One row of machines showed obvious damage, over at the west side where the extraction ducts came in from Viscose Alley. The factory alarm was just above Tommy's head and he stepped over the barrier to get away from it and gain a better view.

He saw three first aiders bending over a couple of men and removing their eye-shields. Welders, it looked like. Tommy realised that there was more damage here than he could have achieved on his own, if he'd really wanted it. Recently, the guilt he'd been feeling... well he was thankful he'd held off telling anyone, including Jacko. *Especially* Jacko.

A fire steward opened the door and released the workers' screams. The factory bellowed on alone until Tommy's ears registered a change: the warp of Atherton's alarm beginning to blend with the weft of emergency vehicles outside.

Mr P was alone in the Lab when Tommy returned. He was instructed to evacuate immediately and meet at the assembly point in the main car park.

Tommy tried to take the instruction in. He'd just been told to cross a threshold he'd successfully avoided for almost two months. The anguish of the injured welders fell from his mind. When Sunehri had waved to him after the performance she'd gone through that exit. He hadn't seen her since.

But he had no choice. From the car park Tommy counted eight fire engines clustered below the blaze, their jets spewing water over amber flames that shot from the roof. Two ambulances sped along the wide sweep of Viscose Alley and their stretchers were immediately unloaded.

Melville came to stand alongside.

'What a stink!' Tommy shouted in his ear.

'Hope you're not referring to me?' It was Fons.

'And rutting stags is a bit minor with all this going on, eh? Reckon it's that roof covering,' Melville said above the noise, looking at Fons, 'the smell.'

A group of workers filed ahead as instructed, including Jean Crossthwaite, and Tommy and Melville were caught in the flow. When Fons was out of earshot Melville asked Tommy, 'What is it with you two? Fighting over a lass or something?'

'Not any longer.' Tommy said, surprised by his public admission.

'What was that you said?'

Tommy felt relieved that Melville hadn't heard.

They watched the rafters reveal themselves to the sky as flecks of burnt materials floated down like papery black snow. Tommy wondered what the spinners would do tomorrow. A roof that size couldn't be re-built in a week or even a month. He'd ask Pieter Janssen about it.

Mr Atherton arrived with the Technical and Production Managers and they walked round the edge of the affected building. Tommy thought that the bloke pointing and talking must be a senior officer from the Fire Station. They were all keeping their distance, and they all looked perfectly grim. Tommy knew that stopping the machines was unacceptable, so the boss must be thinking of ways to get the operatives inside and the production back on track. He wondered how he'd feel if it was an O'Reilly family business going up in flames. Tasteless Ornaments Ltd? *Good riddance.*

The medical crew emerged with two welders on stretchers, drips swinging. 'Know them, Mel?'

'One's Mouji I think. Don't recognise the other.'

Two ambulances went off with their sirens blaring, which left another three standing on the tarmac. Eventually the word went round that all the spinners were being sent home. What surprised everyone was that they'd also been instructed to report for work tomorrow as usual.

In spite of there being plenty of points round the factory and as much water as might need to be drawn from the underground lake, the blaze was still going two hours later.

Eventually, Mr Postlethwaite said they could return to their work. Not much was done for the rest of the day though, except speculating on how the fire had started. The favourite theory was that chemicals in the Viscose Department had somehow caught fire.

That night Tommy's mind was racing. He woke up shouting, saw his dad by his bed, felt him shaking his arm gently, heard him ask if he was all right.

Tommy said he was, but once on his own again he rammed huge balls of toilet paper in his ears. He wondered whether Jamelia Jones had heard his shouts through the wall - hard not to, in a weavers' terrace.

And had she said anything about him calling round in the middle of the night?

Tommy pressed his hands to his ears to try and quieten the terror.

30

The Surgery

Next morning, after cycling past the barrier at the gatehouse and ignoring Mr Embley, Tommy went straight for the site of the fire. He was surprised to see one end of the roof still smouldering and a hose sending a steady arc of water to finish the dampening down.

He couldn't resist calling in at the Surgery. If he discovered something the Spectre didn't know, it would be worth a reprimand for being late.

Nurse Smith looked up as Tommy went in. 'See who we've got here.'

Tommy picked up a roll of bandage and started fiddling with it. The crepe soon got out of control, and after struggling to catch the ends the whole lot unravelled to the floor.

Nurse Smith corralled the tangled bandages and threw them in the bin. 'Helpful contribution that, Tommy. It's lucky we're limited to a few cases of shock and minor cuts, or with trouble like you around supplies would be running low.'

Tommy heard footsteps and shuffling, and Nurse Appleforth poked her head through the gap in a plastic curtain. 'Tommy, escaped the fire then.'

'Hiya Lucy, you look shattered.'

'Thanks for that. Well, I was up all last night in case I was needed, and I'm on days this week so I'm still here.'

Tommy sat on the bed. 'Bit of a raw deal if you ask me.'

Nurse Appleforth drew the curtain fully. 'Not as bad as those welders. Anyhow, who's asking you? And why aren't you at work already?'

Tommy was thinking, *anything new?* He asked, 'How are they doing?'

'Both still in intensive care,' Nurse Appleforth said. 'Serious burns, not life-threatening thank goodness.'

'Any idea how it happened?'

'Fraid not, Tommy,' the nurse said.

'You know they always keep the Carbon Disulphide and Dimethylamine separate, on the other side of Viscose Alley?'

Nurse Smith coughed and looked at Lucy. 'Not really.'

'Maybe the chemicals bridged the two parts of the factory. You get Dimethylamine in volcanic eruptions, you know.'

Nurse Smith pulled a face. 'Well, no doubt they'll be doing a full investigation.'

'Maybe you're running it, Detective O'Reilly?' Lucy Appleforth said. 'I wouldn't put it past you.'

'Better be going then. Bye, Lucy. Bye, Nurse Smith.'

The nurses waved. Before the door had fully closed Tommy heard what they were saying about him, and there were no surprises. He teazed his sideburns as he walked, bringing the hairs to a neat point above the line of his jaw. He felt positive about his new look. It was definitely coming along.

Sort of on the way to the Lab he called in to the Spinning department to see the damage from inside. He'd expected the mood to be quiet, depressed, taking stock, but in spite of the residual smell of burning, it was more like Preston railway station in holiday week. Qasim came straight over and pointed to a group of workers in luminous tabards. 'Outside contractors. Mr Atherton brought them in overnight. He'll be paying over the odds, mind, but they'll make it safe. We're in already, so there's that.'

Tommy looked up. 'There's a gigantic hole in the roof!'

Qasim nodded. 'See, they've rigged up some lighting and started on the scaffolding. The Heavy Gang are giving us a hand sorting things.'

Ginger traipsed across with his broom, sweat beading on his forehead. 'Sweeping's tougher than spinning, Tommy boy. Lazy boy, you are.' He looked round. 'Only one end of the department's out of bounds, so not bad going.'

'Not bad going,' Qasim echoed. 'See where the extraction ducting joins to the Viscose? The fire started with...'

'A welding spark it was,' Ginger cut in.

Tommy had never thought about a welding spark destroying a factory. He felt something on his cheek. Rain was coming through the roof. It wasn't normal. 'What're they doing about the roof then?'

'Complete rebuild,' Qasim explained. 'Manager told us it'd take a couple of months, maybe more. Surveyors're coming later, foreman said.'

Ginger laid his broom against the wall and walked off. 'Where's them hats they said they'd bring us when the weather turned? First day, too.'

Qasim straightened. 'Need to be getting going.'

Tommy gave him a sympathetic look and the spinner whispered, 'It's extra pay for doing with no roof. Me and the missus might book a cruise!'

'It's not *that* much is it, enough to cover a cruise?'

'Well Tommy, depends how long we'll be working under the stars. See, Lori's aunty's left us something in her will and she was one of them sort with no childer of her own, worked all her working life, there was never owt in t'fridge when you went round. What was she saving up for?'

Tommy laughed. 'For you to go on an expensive holiday, that's what.'

Qasim joined Ginger and the line of spinners wearing waterproof hats and coats and working at the undamaged machines while contractors cleared up around them. Tommy was glad not to be in their gumboots - same work, same hours, no roof.

Unlike the seamless way one process morphed into the next at Atherton's and the way most workers seemed to think about their lives, Tommy found it easier to cope if he split his life into chunks:

> Work: Trying out Dicky N's new valve system when
> he could get away with it (since new machines got
> installed about every decade here), a short chat with
> the girls in the Cake Wrapping (it used to be the
> Coning), watching the Pfleiderers doing their business
> (he could watch that all day)

<u>Weekdays at home</u>: Washing-up, sweeping the yard using dogsbody training, reading, football while the evenings were still light enough.

<u>Weekends</u>: Training with Jacko, reading *The Iliad* or Dickens or Emily Dickinson, renewing the loan for *Love on the Dole* and saving up for a personal copy by not going to the Club, pestering the local librarian about why they stocked *Pakistan Today* published in 1947 and a concise Urdu-English dictionary and pretty much nothing else on the subject.

As Tommy sat down at the bench, his mam's latest probing question flew into his head: *What did he want for his birthday tea?* Lamb hotpot was all he could think of. They hadn't had that for ages. He could hardly contain his excitement.

The manager had told everyone there was to be a write-up in the paper about the making of the special shade and flags. Soon Glory Gold would be decorating the civic buildings, and Sunehri wouldn't know a thing about it. He might not bother with the processions. He could wait another twenty years for a ceremony, but not for Sunehri Saleem. His grandma went on about the War delaying the '42 Guild and how the next one in 1952 had set the celebrations on a fresh footing. It sounded like nostalgic rubbish to Tommy.

During the day he made sure Victor heard the news directly from his mouth that there was to be extra pay for the spinners because of working conditions. The Spectre didn't appear to be listening, but Tommy knew he was by the stillness on his face.

147

Over the weeks more came out about the fire, though not much more than had already been surmised through factory gossip. Gas fumes had collected in the duct joining the Viscose and the Spinning departments, and when the welders had started a repair job sparks from a welding torch had ignited the chemicals, sending the flames shooting back to the west end. The spread to the Acid storeroom was a clean-up job for the specialist fire crew. Everything was under control.

One day when Tommy was sitting alone at his favourite canteen table, Naseem and Harry walked in. He overheard them talking about Sunehri and her mam, how they were both fine and healthy and how they'd be staying in Pakistan.

So he'd guessed right - Sunehri was there!

What next? Was she staying forever?

And thinking about it, why were they going on about the health of two perfectly healthy individuals?

Because Sunehri was healthy enough to be married?

There could be no other explanation - Tahira's wedding was long gone.

Tommy stared at his cheese and onion pasty until it was cold and he thought better of finishing his drink when he saw the skin across the top. But he wouldn't cave in. The factory fire had given him, what? A sense of perspective wasn't exactly how he'd describe it, and it wasn't taking the strength of his dad's argument either, about making the most of every day. That was far too corny. The fire had changed him, and one day he might be able to put a finger on exactly how.

31

Goosnargh

At the weekend, midday on the dot, a visitor was shown into the front room by Tommy's dad. He introduced her as Eliza. Tommy was already sitting at the table as instructed, smiling as instructed. His mam said a brief hello then retreated.

Tommy had only just become aware of the following information, through hearing raised voices in the kitchen: Jamelia had decided that having everyone round the table last time was the reason the arrangement had flopped. His dad had muttered, 'The lad's personal business is his business. He'll be twenty soon.' Tommy had decided to go along with a second arrangement for the sport.

He watched his dad point to one of two chairs tucked under the table and enjoyed seeing the visitor make a swift crossing.

First, Tommy nodded at Eliza like a bulldog on a dashboard. Second, he lit a cigarette. His mam didn't mind him smoking anywhere except at the table. Tommy removed his cup from the pretty lavender saucer and flicked ash into it.

Eliza placed her shiny handbag on top of the table, an unusual move in the O'Reilly house. She noticed Tommy staring at it, so placed the handbag by her feet. After a few moments she brought it to her lap, undid the clasp and took out a paper bag printed with the words *Bessie's Bakery at Goosnargh*.

Tommy had always considered the faded garlands on the front of bakery bags a lie to the butter or steak pies, lard pastry cases, the vanilla slices and other sickly-sweet stuff his mam and half the neighbourhood were partial to.

'That's where you're from, is it?' he asked.

Eliza nodded. 'I work in the chemist's, next to the doctor's.'

Tommy grabbed the bag. Though small, it felt heavy, and he thought of unwanted kittens on a final trip to the canal, then of the Pfleiderers, grinding. He untwisted both corners of the silky paper bag and looked inside. 'Goosnargh cakes!' He beamed at their guest. 'My least favourite of all cakes. Congratulations.'

Mrs O'Reilly came in and scowled at the ash scarring one of her best saucers. 'Yer needn't have, Eliza.'

'Is the Goosnargh cake, do you think, closer to the biscuit as a species?' Tommy asked. 'Mam, what do you think?'

She stood motionless near the table holding the teapot. Eventually she plonked the pot down and placed a pale disk of shortcake with heavy sugar dusting on the two plates.

'Won't you and Mr O'Reilly be having one?' Eliza asked.

'Later, ta love.'

'Come out Annie, or sit down or summat,' Frank said through the hinges of the kitchen door.

Annie departed and Eliza re-twisted the corners of the bakery bag. She left it at the edge of the table, spare Goosnargh cakes inside. She snapped her handbag shut and put it by her feet.

The silver cake tray, centrepiece of the table, was packed to the rafters. Home-made chocolate cornflakes on the top tier were complemented by two misshapen coconut volcanoes

150

featuring coconut strands glued on with raspberry jam. The bottom layer had neatly-cut triangles of egg and cress. Tommy calculated that three, maybe more like four, would make a normal-sized sandwich.

He pointed at the tallest volcano. 'Do you want that one Eliza, before it erupts?'

She gave him a knowing look and sniggered.

Tommy picked up his Goosnargh cake from the little bone china plate and took a breath. Eliza watched, fascinated, as he lifted the cake to his mouth and sent a strong gust of air across the top.

Since she was sitting opposite, caster sugar showered over her. Eliza blinked rapidly.

Tommy was surprised to find that she wasn't swearing at him. 'I don't understand why they have to go and lather it on like that!' He banged the table, making the teacups and cutlery jump. 'And now I've gone and wasted it when we could have used it in our drinks.' Tommy noticed his mam. 'Stopping or flitting?'

Annie snatched the dustpan and brush from her husband. It was a three-part operation. First Eliza patted the fine white granules from her hair and blouse, then Annie swept the tablecloth, and finally she brushed the carpet as best she could without moving the table and chairs.

'Pleased to meet you, lass,' Frank O'Reilly said as he lifted his cap from the hook in the vestibule. 'Let's see if we can't put a few bets on to win and cheer everyone up.'

Tommy re-opened the bakery bag and shook it until the remaining sugar had congregated in one corner. He poured a cup of tea for himself and tipped the sugar in, stirring vigorously. 'Nothing to worry about - there's enough after all.'

When Eliza said she needed to go, his first thought was *Sunehri* and the number of times she'd said the same thing. *Main nay jana hay.* More than anything, he wanted Eliza to stay.

Annie said goodbye and Eliza made for the door.

Tommy offered to walk her to the bus stop, and this appeared to surprise his mam more than her guest.

'It's two buses,' Eliza said as they walked along. 'One to Preston, one from Preston to Goosnargh.'

'Suppose it is,' Tommy said. 'You carried them a long way, those really heavy cakes. Like Goosnargh cakes do you?'

She curled her lip.

Tommy smiled. 'There's enough sugar for a stable-full of horsey treats for a year.'

Eliza looked into his blue eyes. 'Or a bus-full of people suffering from diabetes.'

He kept a straight face.

'I was told to bring them with us.' Eliza put her hands on her hips. 'It was my mum and dad's fault, that.'

'Nah, it's my mam's. She'll get over it.'

'And Jamelia's,' said Eliza. 'For setting it up. Us up.'

They both knew it was nearly one hundred per cent Tommy's fault and that he was sorry for it.

'What do you do at this chemist's, then?'

'Collect the prescriptions, give the checked medicines out to patients, stack the shelves.'

They waited for the traffic lights to change.

'Some of the patients, we should sell them string bags.'

'What for?'

'It's a whole shopping list,' Eliza explained. 'Boxes and bottles of tablets, tubes of cream, corn plasters, insoles for de-odourising your feet, eiderdowns, jumping kangaroos, jars of slugs with roasted turnips - that's for treating constipation.'

'Hypochondriacs the lot of them,' he said, without smiling.

'Some, maybe. I wouldn't like to say.'

'I'm a hypochondriac.'

Eliza stopped. 'Are you?'

'Yeah, I've been to loads of doctors and it's the same story every time. There's only one cure, apparently.'

'For what?'

'I just told you - I'm a hypochondriac. There's a single cure for my many, many illnesses.'

'What's that?'

'Sex.'

Eliza burst out laughing.

Tommy glanced his hand off hers as they set off walking again. He was testing her reaction. Sunehri was the one who had done it to him, before.

By the time he had dropped Eliza at the stop and arrived back in his road, his mood had improved. That kiss before she'd climbed on the bus, it wasn't bad, not bad at all. Yet when all your thoughts lead to someone else... Eliza would have said yes to meeting up again, but that wasn't going to give either of them what they wanted. He certainly didn't favour Jamelia sticking her nose in any further than she'd already stuck it.

Tommy's mam was waiting for him with a part-eaten Goosnargh cake in her hand and a sugar-encrusted mouth. 'I knew what to expect about teenagers, but yer quite something on yer own, son.'

Annie looked at his jet black hair, good skin like Frank's, freckles like Frank. 'It'll happen,' she said. 'A good-looking lad and yer in trouble, no mistake. Dad'll be in soon enough.' She kissed Tommy gently on his forehead.

'Sorry, Mam,' he said when she was out of earshot.

The thought of being left alone felt like a great relief. Then Tommy wanted his dad to come back. Anything but the sound of... *What was that crashing round his head?*

There was a knock.

'Mam!' Tommy called.

Annie went to get it.

'I did mean to tell yer, Annie,' Jamelia said quietly from the front step. 'There's not been the opportunity. Is Tommy in?'

'Want to talk to him?'

Jamelia lowered her voice still further, although not enough to prevent Tommy from hearing. 'It's all right, dear, it's well... he came round. I was going to say, but it went clear out of my mind.'

'Anything wrong with Tommy coming round, Jamelia?'

'Yer not getting my drift. It was close on two in the morning and he was wearing pyjamas and knocking so loud I thought he must be in some kind of trouble.'

'Was he?'

'Well, dear, I don't really think so because you and Frank came back from holiday next day and when I seen him after, he looked no glummer than usual, fer someone his age.'

'I didn't hear nowt about that.'

'I seen him from up top, dear. He stood there no longer than a minute, I'd say.'

'Well, if it weren't no longer than a minute I suppose it weren't serious.'

'But Annie... and I need to ask how it went with, *you know*, don't I. Oh, it'll save.'

'It will,' said Annie, and she closed the door.

32

A Masterpiece

August rolled on and Tommy gave up smoking, just like that. Losing cigarette breaks didn't mean an end to infuriating the Spectre, though. Tommy would leave unannounced whilst making sure he went beyond the requirements of his job. He'd heard Victor putting in a complaint last week but there had been no comeback, and he hadn't been in a fight for yonks.

Today, at a carefully chosen moment when Victor dipped into the darkroom, Tommy went up the half-stairs to the Spinning.

He nodded at Vivian, Parwez, Jack, Tony Tubbs and Qasim stationed at the machines numbered 125 to 159 that spun the pigmented yarn Tommy always worked on, five machines to a row, 102 ends on a machine, 51 ends to a side.

In the whole of the department ten machines spun tyre yarn, some spun dyed yarn, while others made matt yarn by adding titanium dioxide. The rest of the spinning machines produced non-pigmented yarn, which was sold on cakes or cones for other factories to weave, or on cakes for dyeing when customers didn't require the more permanent pigments. It was busy, chaotic, orderly and productive here, and it was a good place to run away to.

Tommy stood by machine number 159, its common cast-iron feed pipe bringing the spinning-viscose up from the de-aeration tanks in the Caves. In his four years he'd learnt that air bubbles caused yarn breakages when spun, and he knew about removing undissolved cellulose fibres by filtration and he understood why viscose was pumped through presses clad in fine calico and rougher cloths, cloths that were washed and re-used and that came in handy when clumsy trainees stood on pigment drums and needed wiping down in the nude. But he didn't understand about Sunehri.

The rotten egg smell in the Spinning didn't usually bother him as much as the smell in the Churn Room. Today, although he knew the importance of having a 10% sulphuric acid bath to neutralise the caustic soda in the viscose, the smell wafting from the open windows of the spinning machine made him wrinkle his nose. *He must be getting soft.*

He lounged by the gear pumps, thinking about the golden-coloured liquid that was being driven through the filter and then through the tiny holes of the jet. Although it was the spitting image of honey, if Tommy had been able to stick his finger in the flow of viscose, the caustic soda would have burned his tongue. He knew that the chain molecules must be the perfect length for making stretchable yarn, sodium sulphate slowing the precipitation enough for the fibres to regenerate continuously into solid threads of artificial silk right in front of his eyes.

Liquid to solid, like alchemy, like that Dr Dee only better.

Maybe.

But the chemical picture was the most compelling part for Tommy because it wasn't common knowledge. He was happy to tell anyone who'd give him ear-time that, after reacting with the CS_2 in the churns, the alk-cell was more accurately described as xanthate cellulose, then when that was dissolved in caustic soda it became viscose and...

$$H_2SO_4 + NaOH/Cell/Xanthate = Cellulose + Na_2SO_4 + H_2O + H_2S$$

Sulphuric Acid + Sodium Hydroxide/Cellulose/Xanthate =
Cellulose + Sodium Sulphate + Water + Hydrogen Sulphide (gas)

Mr P and Melville, Naseem, Harry, Dicky N, Roman, Jean, even Victor, he had to admit, they'd all taught him parts of the story, and Tommy had managed to bring the pieces together. He sensed that this knowledge was worth something, but right now its full value wasn't obvious. Maybe he'd set up his own artificial silk factory, dozens of factories, travel the world...

'What's up? Share the joke?'

'Nothing much. Hey, Qasim, been on that cruise yet?'

'Believe it or not, we went along the coast, sailed down the coast. We'd go again tomorrow. I wouldn't want another fire to pay for it though. We topped up with a few hundred from Lori's aunty, so it was good timing. Not for her.'

'You deserved it, the lot of you. Better to use it for something than let it sit.'

The spinner returned to his work, leaving Tommy feeling pathetic for not having left Preston in over a year.

Wadi passed by on his way to the Jet Room and Tommy caught his attention. 'Got over the shock yet?'

The spinner flinched. 'Nurse Appleforth instead of Gary Booth might have helped.'

'She's got a brain on her as well, you know.'

Tommy traced the continuous movement of the non-pigmented, off-white thread passing over and round a bottom godet, to be taken up and round a top godet. He watched both godets cleverly revolving at slightly different speeds to stretch and strengthen the yarn by aligning the cellulose in the viscose before it was fully precipitated. He followed the thread's line through the up-down, up-down, glass funnels and distribution by centrifugal force, 9,000 revolutions a minute, resulting in a perfectly wound cake of yarn inside every Topham Box. He understood how everyone was joined in a common purpose and how a steady flow was maintained from the point where wood pulp arrived on the branch line to the winding of threads of viscose in a factory whose heart never stopped beating.

Tommy walked to the next row of machines and didn't know how long he was standing there before Vivian came over.

'Doff time - help if you want?'

Tommy nodded, and began lifting the first of ten windows that covered the spinning machines. One of the jets that prevented crystals from forming in the cakes sprayed a mist of water droplets in his face and obscured his view. While Tommy wiped himself, Vivian lifted the first Topham Box off the spindle of the motor then banged it on the edge of the tray to release the cake inside.

Tommy's vision cleared. That shade looked like... he stopped the thought and focused on Vivian tipping the wound cake from the box onto the wooden tray.

The spinner carried on collecting cakes down the line, cakes that would spend time in one of the cabinets lining the walls. In the early days Tommy had stepped inside a cabinet to see what it was like, and last month one had been adapted as a prayer room by the Muslim men who wanted it. They'd laid a patterned carpet. He'd like to see it again, changed, but he didn't even dare ask.

Idzi came in driving a motorised truck with a tall stainless steel drum containing a new batch of part-pigment, part-water made up in the Caves. He steered the truck right at Tommy and left it until the last second before veering off.

Tommy wasn't scared. He was hardly conscious. He watched Idzi stop next to the machines.

'Regular batch of Glory Gold,' Idzi said. 'Third one today.'

Tommy raked his fingers through his hair. 'Mr P says the reps've had no problems selling it. Restricted to selling it abroad for now, a courtesy to the Guild Committee.'

Idzi sniffed. 'That's none of my business.' He dunked the delivery hose from the pump on the Collis into the top of the spinning machine's hopper so that the pigment could be drawn up. 'Staying to watch, since yer created the beauty?'

Tommy knew the next part of the process so well that he gained some satisfaction from visualising the stages: the blade would revolve inside the hopper to keep the pigment from precipitating, the liquid would be metered by a pump so that the correct amount of pigmented viscose was fed to the 102 individual metering pumps and through the candle filters and into the spinning bath to be regenerated as solid thread.

He knew that all right, but he'd forgotten the reason for being here. 'Right,' Tommy said to Idzi before moving off.

Idzi pulled a face and started up a conversation with Vivian,

160

then called over: 'I'll be taking a sample winding from one of these cakes. Pick it up on yer way to the Lab if you've nothing better to do, mate.'

Tommy decided to go and see the spot where the fire had broken out. He found that the only sign the roof had been damaged was its newness compared to all the other surfaces that had been patched over the years. But the wall next to where the extraction ducts came in was more obvious. It had a glossy finish.

Ginger wandered over, stretching his arms and legs. 'All change, eh? Moved the storage tanks, they have.'

'Where to?'

'External building, right round the other side.'

Tommy pointed to the new paint. 'Clive's masterpiece?'

'Sorted the sign too. Permanent.'

Tommy studied the sign for a few moments, then delivered the words like a B-movie actor:

SAFETY FIRST - WELDERS!
DANGER OF EXPLOSION
PERMISSION REQUIRED
REPORT 1ST TO: FIRE STEWARD
OR *SPINNING MANAGER.*

'Get on, Tommy! It was serious, that fire.'

'I was here remember, near as. At least I made you laugh. Right miseryguts you were when you came over.'

Ginger patted Tommy lightly on the back, and left him skirting machine number 160 that was being cannibalised for spares, enabling the other machines to continue producing yarn. *Was there a message in that? Probably not!*

He caught Ginger's eye on the way out and nodded at the long rack of fusty gumboots, a rail above holding a hundred waterproof coats. It reminded him of the cloakroom at his old Grammar School. He wished he was there still, learning French still with Monsieur Dubois and drowning in Mr Southworth's vivid imagination.

Why, apart from Mr P and Sunehri and a handful of others, why was he surrounded by people who didn't care one way or the other about reading books?

'Thought of a use for those yet?' he called to Ginger, pointing out the line of waterproofs. 'Now the roof's mended?' Tommy didn't wait for an answer.

33

The Neighbours

Monday the 4th of September 1972, the day before the Churches' procession. Along with some of the other workers at Atherton's Tommy had managed to get Guild Week off, though the machines never stopped. His holiday had been booked months before, when he'd hoped to spend at least some of it with Sunehri. Now he had nothing planned except a bit of football with Jacko and some of the lads, and reading *The Odyssey* which would take about a week. Aunty Eileen was coming from Ireland to stay with his grandma, and even his cousins Noel and Gerrard were doing something - a two-guitar set at their local.

That morning, his mam had brought back a small box of Union Jacks from the shop. Apparently the new Guild flags were due in tomorrow, delayed, Mr Cuff said, because of high demand and the need for a second impression. His mam reported that Jamelia Jones had informed the shop that she'd never lost sleep over mopers and she wasn't going to start. And that she'd tell anyone, including Gertie Godber, that if anyone gave a lacklustre response to the final decision of having a street party they should keep indoors and watch the telly. And she wasn't quite finished yet, since programmes like *North West Tonight* might well be showing people like us having a tea party, dear. Over breakfast Tommy's mam had labelled him a "Gertie".

As far as he could recall, the menu currently stood at:

- Guild Street Party Menu -

Savouries: fish paste, egg and cress and
Spam sandwiches (Annie O'Reilly had failed to sway the
vote for corned beef),
Butter pies and Steak pies (bought in),
Caribbean chicken and rice, Lancashire hotpot,
garlic & chilli dip

Puddings: battered bananas, home-made ginger cake
(an O'Reilly family recipe),
15 x Coffee Renoirs cut into quarters (Mrs Jay buying
from Round's due to a recent win on the dogs),
lime and strawberry jelly, Cuff's ice cream,
Burfi (Iram Manzoor's recipe - delicious nutty fudge),
Eccles cakes (slabs of dry pastry with squashed ants -
medical advice: swill down with a mug of tea),
Oh, and still on puddings, Tommy hoped *not* to see those
little spongy buttermilk domes, Gulab Jabab, Julab Jaman
or something. Sunehri had brought some to the park.
Verdict: like eating eyeballs.

Drinks: jugs of squash, a fair bit of booze (kept in
Jamelia's front room so as not to offend the teetotallers)

None apart from his mam would have noticed that Tommy hadn't offered any further suggestions.

He was more interested in the guest list. He knew that all the neighbours from two streets on either side had received invitations, and that this included the Saleem household. Round here, it was generations born and died on the same street - the Dohertys, Butts, Godbers, Gornalls Manzoors, McGintys, Eastons, Brethertons, Joneses, Chowdhurys, they'd all share recipes, discover similar spices and methods, mixing Indian and West Indian talk and Urdu and English and Irish after school, at the weekend, in the holidays. For as long as Tommy could remember Jamelia had been the go-between.

At Junior School he'd shouted 'Paki!' a few times when everyone was else was doing it. Was that an excuse? The Pakistani children had shouted something indistinct back, probably an equivalent slur. He'd been too embarrassed to ask Sunehri what it might have been.

All he could remember since then was thinking that languages were for everyone, not only the people who were brought up with them. In the factory people worked side-by-side didn't they, well not top management - which was men with white skin - but most other places, at the launderette, the Post Office, on the bus, in other people's houses. Just not in his house. Tommy had grown up playing with his cousins, who were like him.

It was only this morning that he'd realised his parents might not be around to see the next Guild, and his mind had spun forward to the one after that. In 2012, unless another world war got in the way, he might be drawing a pension. Would he still be living in Preston? Since he didn't know anywhere else, probably. And the big question was: Could that be called living?

What about Sunehri? Her home in England from the age of five always round the corner from him, her dad working on the Dam through her teenage years, near her grandparents and the aunties and uncles and cousins still in Mirpur, her saying how much against their family tradition it was to be separated.

Enough of a family tradition they'd found a nice Pakistani boy for her? Someone who didn't get into fights? Well, she'd done what she'd always wanted - flown across the world. Tommy had never heard that *staying there* was part of the plan. Dark khol lines framing her dark eyes, shiny chains suspended from her nose to a headdress, a costume heavy enough with sequins to make a wedding day - this was the image that filled his mind.

She'd never even come round his house. Not once.

He'd never been round hers.

She'd never invited him.

He'd never invited her.

Tommy looked out. If the weather didn't improve, well, he'd better prepare for increased sightings of long, belted cardigans. The street tea party would go ahead no matter what the weather was like. Sitting at that giant table next to Sunehri Saleem, homes turned inside out, making the world seem different, it would have been perfect.

Yesterday there'd been talk of the neighbours clubbing together for sparklers and walking down to Avenham with the torchlight procession, to watch the fireworks explode across the water by Tram Bridge. He might do that, go on his own. He could take his torch, the charred one under his bed that he hadn't looked at since he'd got it back. *Not that kind of torch!*

He heard Aaron Kellet's bell outside and remembered the old metal bucket his dad had wanted to chuck for ages. He remembered the dull planning meetings held alternate weeks in their front room, where there had been a discussion about using old buckets for party rubbish.

The planning group comprised of Jamelia (of course), his mam, Harry Manzoor, Falak Butt and Mrs Cuff. At last week's meeting they had finally decided how to match up the tables that had been offered, so that one edge wasn't too much lower or higher than the next. It was a giant jigsaw puzzle and together they'd worked out the correct height at one end of the street for the lankiest legs to fit under, his dad's, and the correct height at the other end to suit the children. At the shop Gertie Godber had cautioned Mrs Cuff against having bowls of jelly too far down the table, especially if it wasn't properly set like Annie O'Reilly tended to make it. Tommy sensed that any initial embarrassment about displaying private tables in public, with all their scratches, peeled veneer and burn marks, had waned.

At the point when he got to thinking about the quiet, dead house round the corner, Tommy O'Reilly was already tearing his *Happy Cavalcade* poster to shreds, and Sunehri Saleem was already moving to her window to see what was going on in the street.

Raga-Bo-o-o-o-o-ne.

34

Kapray aur Hadiyaan

Sunehri decided to watch Mr Kellet with his ramshackle cart, anything but unpacking her suitcase. They had travelled on the coach from London yesterday and the long flight had given her an excuse to sit in bed reading tatty copies of Lalleshwari's *vakhs* and her favourite Emily Dickinson poems, letting the day ebb, some light snacks to eat - that's all she'd wanted, though not all that she needed.

It was about an hour until tea, as her maa had just called up to remind her, so there was an expectation that the washing piles would be sorted.

Why did her parents have to come and live in a place that was so wet? She wondered if the processions would be cancelled. If the weather cleared she would go and watch the marching bands, alone if needs be.

Mr Kellet rang his bell again then gave a shortened call, 'RgBnn!' Sunehri wiped the condensation to get a better view of the man who Tommy said used to be good friends with his granddad – they had been at school together.

She knew the call well enough by now, but she hadn't thought about the separate words before, 'rags and bones'. On a whim she decided she'd test them out: *kapray aur hadiyaan kapray aur hadiyaan kapray aur...* and ended up with a dizzy tongue. The Urdu didn't sound right. She might ask her maa.

Tommy had told her that Mr Kellet was not looking for rags because they fetched far less than metal - whether rusty or not - unless the clothes, tablecloths or whatever could be sold on complete, to be used again. Washing machines, metal rods, pipes left over from plumbing jobs and bicycles were welcome. Once there had been a scooter that looked so twisted, a trip to the hospital must have come into the story somewhere. She had never heard it.

That was the thing about the cart - it told a partial story. There had been a table with not enough legs to hold it up. She knew the wood would make useful kindling through the winter, but worried that the memories of the conversations and meals had over it would be lost.

Tommy had been clear about the metal, that Mr Kellet hoped to sell it for *good money*, that was how you said it. More often than not Sunehri had seen items move from the top of the cart to the top of the tower in Mr Kellet's yard. She'd noticed yesterday coming from the station that the tower had grown like Jack's beanstalk while they were away.

Tommy had also told her that bones were not welcome unless there was a bit of mutton on for Racer. She remembered the dog riding in the cart last year, yapping when the bell was rung, setting the local strays off. Maybe Mr Kellet enjoyed the amplified advertising. She had never seen his pet reprimanded. Racer was too old to be joggled over the wheels now, so Mr Kellet took him to Tommy's grandma's for a *change of scene* when he went on his rounds.

A change of scene.

She would like to meet Racer, and especially she would like to meet Tommy's family. He had never invited her, but she did understand. She did.

Sunehri heard the bang of two sets of cutlery and two plates on the table downstairs. She wasn't looking forward to mealtime. She wiped the cold windowpane with her cardigan sleeve and saw that the cart was a moving picture gallery enabling neighbours to weigh the objects and judge them. As far as Sunehri knew, her maa had never donated anything. She was a private person. It was one of their problems.

Although he moved slowly because of a limp, it seemed to Sunehri that Mr Kellet moved too quickly for someone who did have something to clear out. Once or twice she'd seen people emerging after his cart had gone into Skeffington Road where Tommy lived, the house with the tall end wall that connected his mam permanently to the mill where she worked. To Sunehri that was not a comforting thought.

She watched the carrier shuffle under the arch of Mrs Easton's ginnel and put his hand to the side of his head. A flicker of *naraanji* lit the soggy air. Sunehri had always been fascinated by people who smoked. None of her family did. She didn't like the smell on Tommy's breath but she did like the way he hid cigarettes above one ear and challenged her to guess which one.

What was he doing this very minute?

She must stop asking herself things she couldn't know.

Sunehri's mind took her back to a day trip after finishing school and before starting at Atherton's. Her maa had not

170

wanted her to go off, whereas Sunehri was desperate to explore before being trapped by a job. It was also a birthday treat. She had caught the bus to Southport.

Just being on the bus was a welcome escape from her maa's guilt and soul-searching, the non-stop worrying about whether she should have come back to Preston when Abbu must always be so far away for his work.

Abbu...

But that warm September day last year, paying for her ticket, sitting on the top deck of the bus for the long, straight journey west, it had felt to Sunehri like she was as free as a bird... *Woe eik chiriya ki tara azzad thee.* Most Pakistani girls her age had much less freedom, but she didn't worry about them that day.

The bus had dropped her close to the sea wall, and she'd been amazed by the miles and miles of Southport sand with no sign of the sea. She'd walked down the cement steps, removed her shoes, rolled up the bottoms of her silk trousers - not too far - and enjoyed the sensation of coolness and acceptance on the soles of her tentative feet. Attaching herself to the beach seemed much more pleasant than spinning round the coast road like all those drivers. Maybe they never got out of their cars.

That day she had seen old people walking dogs and children tipping sand buckets - one like a castle, another like a jelly mould. It was not something she had experienced. At a suitable distance she had watched another family make a huge sand fortress and a moat that would stay free of the damp that constantly grew under her bedroom window. On this beach at Southport it was the wind not the water that would pull a

171

fortification apart, grain by grain. After admiring the tiny pieces of glass lifting from the beach like opaque bubbles she'd felt compelled to hurry her sandwiches before the sand could sneak inside.

She really liked that trip and she would do it again. The bus fare wasn't even that dear. She would take her maa next time if she wasn't being naggy.

On the way to the bus stop a cloud had made an enormous shadow on the smooth sand. At first she'd watched its slow-moving shape, then on an impulse she'd dug a hole in the sand with her heel, grinding it down, pressing hard, pushing it down with her whole body.

Then the waiting. For what? Other kinds of shadow shapes forming and passing her by in an endless cycle? She had looked far out to the horizon and waited, not for the sea-swell.

The Express bus to Preston was about to leave! She'd raced to the steps, dusted the sand from between her toes, pulled on her shoes and arrived at the stop as the bus was drawing away. The driver had seen her in the mirror and stopped. Her scarf got trapped and he re-opened the doors. He apologised, she apologised.

Sitting on the bus she'd wondered what life would be like once she started at Atherton's. She knew a few things from Tahira, and Parvin would be starting before Christmas, so it would probably be all right, three cousins together. It had been all right.

Precious memories now flowed from the days before Tahira's wedding, her maa and Abbu together, seeming happy. She tried to think of the faces of her family in Mirpur, but Tommy kept intruding, his eyes the colour of blue poppies from the mountains or the blue of Mirpur Lake, his funny hair with all that lotion to keep it away from his forehead, his lips, the fact that she had not said goodbye to him.

And here she was in England again after many weeks away, after expecting to be away for one. It was usually her and her maa in Preston, but this time when they left Pakistan to come here it had felt so much worse.

That photograph on her bedside table... of course she missed her father, more than ever.

Abbu. Daddy.

She wished, more than wished if there was such a thing, that he'd stayed here and worked, stayed here with them and never taken that other job.

'Raga-Bo-o-o-ne!' No hand bell this time. Sunehri saw that the carrier hung his head in a way that expected nothing of interest to appear. She remembered the carts at home taking reddish-brown pots to market, their hard clay clonking together as the cart went over bumps, their beautiful scalloped edges like her maa's pastry crusts. And the stalls of walnuts, cherries, apricots, mangoes - she especially loved mangoes, probably because there were so few places you could buy them here, and nowhere at all to buy her naani's *chai* milk tea made with crushed almonds from the trees near the house in Mirpur.

Her Uncle Ghusun often carried timbers to sell: fir, deodar, chir pine, and the pine's resin for making soaps. Sometimes he'd have maize, barley, millet, and little hessian bags of herbs for medicine. On special occasions he brought animals like grey goral, snow pheasant in winter, and sheep's hide sacks for grain and butter-making containers. And as soon as they were finished he'd sell the hand-woven baskets and blankets made by her aunty and cousins and an old neighbour.

Only last week Sunehri had travelled on the cart admiring the weaving her naani had done on her small loom. *Deep ochre, vermilion, azure...* she loved the sounds of these English names for the dyes, shades that found their way into the little tassels made by her young cousins Karida and Dalal to bring on their weaving skills.

That day at market the word had gone round that two dhurries woven by her naani were arriving. No sooner had the cart been set down than the rugs were sold. Gone. On her last trip home Sunehri had made a few of the little tassels using the hand-dyed wools. How crude they had looked, unsold on the cart, compared to her naani's clever, ancient weaving.

Sunehri looked out again for Mr Kellet. Gone too. Perhaps he was more of a collector than a carrier. Her family couldn't afford to collect things they didn't need, but Mr Kellet didn't seem rich. Did the profits from rags and bones made him richer or poorer than the neighbours who gave him goods to trade?

She looked at the picture of the minarets on her wall, their pointed hats peeping through the lake like a fairytale, when the rest of the year the curved stones would be hidden by water. Maybe it was tiredness, but instead of water, now she saw sweeping green valleys with maize crops and mango groves and apple trees.

Since the flooding, some of the trees on higher ground had survived, but most had perished for the sake of generating energy. So, were the memories of climbing forgotten when no trees were there to remind people they had climbed as children and picked the fruits?

Mostly, she could only recall that old home through a few photographs and the perspectives of her maa and abbu, and the stories her family told about Old Mirpur. She had not walked those streets after Mangla Lake was formed. How could she?

And she didn't have a single photograph of Tommy.

Sunehri faced the ugly suitcase sprawled open on the bed. It was lucky she had her old job back. She liked the girls and it got her out of the house. The work was not challenging and some days it was actually very boring. The pay was not much but it was important, especially now.

To be truthful, she was returning for Tommy. She feared he might not understand.

35

Plague Cart

Tommy looked down on the handcart arriving in his street. Nobody would defend its split wood and threadbare paint, the many layered colours from previous years breaking through, a home for woodlice and roach, probably a few millipedes. He'd discovered the power of millipedes when he'd dropped one down his mam's dress during a boring school holiday. He wondered if any of Aaron's insect passengers still had their full quota of legs, then whether Aaron's ancestors were resistant to the plague. The same cart might have carried dead friends and neighbours to the boundary of Priest's Town - bent, swollen bodies then, deformed metal now. The handle-less bucket could stay in the yard for another week, until after the street party.

Ignoring the wreck of his room, Tommy sat at his dressing table. He was looking quite good, with better cheekbones than Elvis now that the singer had put on weight... *walk down lonely street...* Tommy smoothed his sideburns and noticed a few stray hairs that needed nicking with a razor. Scissors might be faster. He opened the top drawer and froze.

There was the little plastic bag with its twist of golden-coloured yarn. What shocked him most was that he'd forgotten he'd put it there.

36

Tea at the Saleems'

The sound of clattering plates brought Sunehri to the present, and she sighed at the sight of the folded, dirty clothes. Why did she have to comply with her maa's annoying rule? Folded clothes fitted into the space better, but there was plenty of room for two sets of clothes in their elephant of a suitcase that had been bought for three people to use.

She remembered her promise to Tahira about the wedding photos. Although the quality would not be good on that little throwaway camera from the airport, she would still take it to the shop tomorrow as planned. The previous roll she'd processed was three years ago, after her last visit to Mirpur.

With that thought, Sunehri wanted to speak to Tahira immediately. She might be able to get away with using the phone while her maa was being noisy in the kitchen, but she knew that the telephone bill would not hide any secrets. Maybe when she had earned her first pay packet from the factory? She would see.

Pushed down each side of the suitcase was a pair of *jutay* wrapped in newspaper. On top of the folded pile were her maa's *shalwar*, the awful ones in shades of pink that Sunehri had tried to persuade her not to take. Underneath, she saw what she did not wish to see: the two new *kameezain* still in their bags, bought by her father for when he next came on holiday to Preston.

And there was the tassel she had made using Tommy's favourite reds and golds. She blushed to think of that last time in their den, when she'd unbuttoned his shirt.

Her maa's voice called up:
   Chai tayaar hay!
   (Tea's ready!)

The front door went. Sunehri stood on the landing to listen.

   Oh, tum in sharatiyoon ko lay aaee ho!
   (Oh, you brought the little monsters, did you!)

   Umair aur Yasir, tum donoon kahan chupey hoay thay?
   (Umair and Yasir, where were you two hiding, then?)

   Humarey saath khana kha rahay ho?
   (Are you eating with us?)

   Kaafi hay. Thair jao khanay kay liyaay...
   (We have plenty. Stay to eat...)

   Sunehri, dhonay walay kapray bhi tum nay tiyar kar diaya hain, baad main may un ko dho doon gi?
   (Sunehri, have you sorted the washing, so that I can put a wash on later?)

Yay ganday kapray nikal rahi thi wo humarey wapis aanay par.
(She's been sorting out the dirty washing from our trip you know.)

Sunehri, nichay aajao, issay pehlay kay khana thanda hoe jaayay.
(Sunehri, come down before the food goes cold.)

Sunehri closed the bedroom door and went down to greet her Aunties Falak and Iram and her three cousins. She hugged Parvin, desperately wanting to ask her about Tommy, but the food was already being served.

After eating, Ayesha Saleem saw that the rain had stopped so she shooed the children out to play. To Sunehri's annoyance she and Parvin were included in this instruction, meaning that there was still no chance to talk. When Yasir kicked the ball into the kitchen drain, Sunehri used this as an opportunity to sneak a look through the window. Jamelia Jones had arrived.

Quickly thinking up an excuse should she need one, Sunehri went inside. The first thing she heard was her Aunty Falak saying, 'It is not right to mix it. They will have a hard life if we allow this, Ayesha. Naseem does not necessarily agree with me. I do not know why.'

She heard her Aunty Iram say, 'We know couples where it has not worked because the families, yes, they are so different. Some might be happy if they stay together long enough...'

Sunehri's Aunty Falak interrupted, 'This does not happen. We have not seen this.'

There was the sound of shifting chairs. 'Ayesha? What are you thinking? You talked about it with Rabah, before?' Aunty Iram again.

Sunehri could not see that her maa was keeping her gaze fixed on the small, dark cave of the fireplace. She could hear her silence though.

'Ayesha, there is already enough difficulty for you here. She is your only child...' Aunty Falak's voice faded away and the room fell silent.

Jamelia filled the gap with some gossip about the street tea party menu. She stopped mid-sentence.

Sunehri didn't know what to do. They must have heard her! 'Just getting a drink of water,' she called. 'Yasir is thirsty.'

Jamelia came straight through to the kitchen and wrapped Sunehri in her arms. 'Hello, dear. I'm truly sorry for the both of yer, I truly am.'

37

Kaalaa / Black

Tommy slammed the dressing table drawer shut. He was the happy-go-lucky star of a thrown-together show in a canteen, tragically killed by the grim reaper in the form of a speeding car. And Sunehri? He understood what she used to be. She had moved in to his life a long time ago.

I want you to live in my world. I can't find a way.

If you turned to look at me, any time, I wouldn't ignore you.

Why would I?

Treacle-black plait, kaalaa eyebrows...

You are Sunehri Saleem.

He hadn't been able to find her again, not in his dreams, not even in his waking dreams. *May tum say piyaar karta hoon,* I love you.

Tommy went and mooched about downstairs and was relieved to find a note in his mam's handwriting to say that they would be staying out late.

He went into the rain-soaked yard and managed to hit the privy window with his football first time. Even Jacko might be impressed with that fancy footwork.

38

You

Sunehri had been told by her maa to avoid the fairground, so here she was on Moor Park looking in on the lights and the noise of people enjoying themselves, pushing herself to take another step and go through the perimeter fence. She felt like an outsider, but that wasn't what was stopping her. It was the thought that she would be alone when everyone else was not.

She spotted a familiar face coming her way and panicked, quickly turning so that he would not see her.

It was Alfonso from the Pulp Store - handsome, but trouble. More trouble than Tommy, who was nice trouble!

She set off towards the park feeling lost.

At that same moment, yards away, Tommy and Jacko were stepping off the Dodgems.

Tommy smoothed his hair. 'I'm bored. Three goes is enough.'

Jacko joggled the money in his pocket to calculate how many more rides it equalled. 'Please yourself.'

'Might come to the Rec later. Dunno. See how I feel.'

'Dull - you'll feel dull. Anyway, I'm desperate for a...' Jacko's two-tone whistle moved towards the temporary toilets.

Tommy walked the opposite way, the *I don't know* question

pounding through his body. It was a question as inevitable as coming across Hangface Bazzer by the railway bridge, who whacked people for no good reason. The answers were much harder to come by, and he knew that the compulsion to find them drove the generators and motivated people to count their money for another ride. The more he thought about it, the less he understood what his life was for. A fight wasn't a bad idea. He was quite in the mood for one.

He spotted Fons at the hot dog stand.

Then again, why tramp all the way to the railway bridge when your perfect enemy was within spitting distance?

A sudden breeze made Tommy fasten another button on his jacket. He remembered the oak trees standing guard over their den through autumn, spring, part of summer. He lifted his collar and walked through the metal fence in the direction of the park.

The same breeze broke through a row of trees lining the gravel path where Sunehri was walking. She doubled her cardigan over at the front and tried not to think about Tommy. A week from now she'd be in the Coning department. With such a long gap and only being on the job for six months in the first place, would she still have the knack? What about tying those tricky weavers' knots between the end of one cake and the start of another? What if she tied the knots too big and the yarn broke in the weaving or made slubs? Well, she must try not to worry. That's what her maa kept saying, not that she was a good example. Sunehri's mind moved on to the men's dining room next to the Coning, and it was all about Tommy again.

Screams spluttered from the fairground behind them, and in different areas of the park Tommy and Sunehri both paused, then walked on.

Tommy noticed a few people throwing lazy balls for their dogs, a baby in a pram sucking the corner of a blanket against the cold.

Sunehri stopped to watch a teddy being dropped for a game and retrieved by a parent from the back of a park bench, lads and girls dressed flimsily, all of them going the opposite way.

Any emotion being expressed by anyone else, it was nothing to do with the two people who were walking on separate pathways towards the centre of the park.

As Tommy neared the duck pond he recognised a pattern, a combination of colours, a distinctive outline, a fine scarf draped across her shoulders, floaty trousers drawn in at the ankle with a thick band of shiny material, the buttercup yellow of her long, belted cardigan. He increased his pace, sensing that the whole universe had given him a nudge.

39

A Duck's Life

Sunehri had longed to see Tommy every day. She felt scared now that he was here. In spite of these feelings she walked quickly, needing to be sure it really was him. He looked handsome, though thinner than before. Nearly two months.

She held her tears back then laughed as a cover when they came. 'Tommy, your hair here, round your ears and down your neck! What do you call those, in English?'

They were close enough to touch. 'Sunehri!' he spluttered. 'My... sideburns? These you mean?'

Sunehri tried the word. 'Side burns? You burn the hair? I don't believe it for one minute.' She was joking with him.

Tommy's heart was racing.

'You look different, Tommy.'

'I never thought I'd...'

Sunehri turned to see if anyone was watching. When she turned back she saw his outstretched hand holding some bright thread in a see-through bag.

'Go on,' he said, more loudly than he'd intended.

'Shhh!' Sunehri checked the park again, taking her time.

'It's yours Glory, please.'

She looked into Tommy's face rather than at what was being

offered. *Why was he calling her by that name?*

Tommy's cheeks flushed and he moved closer until there was only space for a butterfly's wing. Then he stepped sideways without warning and bowed to his open hand.

Sunehri liked Tommy playing around, showing off, not caring what people thought - though she cared a great deal.

'Look at it, will you.' Tommy forced the bag into her hand. 'You haven't even looked!'

Sunehri was scanning his face, his strong teeth, he had a tan too, which had brought out more of the freckles. She wondered whether the freckles were his tan. 'I've had no chance to look, Tommy. You have never stopped since you saw me.'

'Stopped what?'

She tentatively took the bag and pulled out a little twist of yarn, knotted at the top. The colour was like a ray of sunshine. She read the label attached by a string. 'Glory Gold? What is this?' She looked across to the ducks preening their tails and thought of Jean Crossthwaite who worked in the Lab, that cotton dress with the pleats that made life appear so orderly when really it was chaotic. Half of her wanted to be with Tommy, the other half was telling her to walk away and carry on walking until she was at home, where her maa could close off the world for her.

Sunehri moved away, though slowly, thinking that a duck's life must be a lot simpler.

Tommy kept one pace behind, confused.

When she spoke again it was without looking at him. 'I was sad when we landed at the airport. The weather was terrible. I was thinking, why should I exchange this for home? It is usually dry there. And when I saw Mr Kellet pushing his cart...'

Tommy cupped his hands round hers. 'Home, Sunehri? Isn't that here?'

She let her hand stay. 'Do not make it hard for me.'

'*Jee haan*,' he replied, nodding. 'It's been a long time. I didn't even know you'd gone, why you'd gone! So what happened, by the exit to the car park, and all those weeks since? What the hell did you think you were playing at?'

'*Mujhay tum bohut yaad aye ttey.*' She brought the golden-coloured silk next to their two faces. 'A ray of sunshine.'

Tommy took some long, deep breaths. He mustn't blow it. 'Sunehri, when you were gone, before, it started before, you know it did. Then you left me and I couldn't stop thinking...'

She remembered the Tommy O'Reilly of years ago in Junior School, chasing Mary McCreedy round the playground. For once Sunehri had decided not to run so fast, to see what would happen. What would happen if he caught her? Tommy didn't notice her that day, or really at all. She thought perhaps it was the difference in their ages. Unless Mary had changed recently, most people would not think of her as chase-able. She felt bad for thinking that. Was it the way Mary kissed? 'How much did you earn this week Tommy O'Reilly?' she asked him.

'How much? At work?' He had missed that, missed how she'd throw in a stray thought, stir things up, test him. 'Well I'm not on shifts yet. It's more money, but you knew that already didn't you, about shifts.'

She glanced a finger down his hand.

'Repping, that's where the money is.' Tommy's voice was shaky. 'Sales is a hard job Mr P says, on the road carrying a case stuffed with samples. I might go in for it later. It might be good.' As he said these words he was thinking that leaving Preston now, even for a second, was the last thing he wanted. He leant against a tree and watched the clouds skid by. 'Mr P, he read something in the *Evening Post* about the way companies promote their products.' He watched Sunehri wrap the golden thread round her finger. 'So, how many years till I'm boss of the whole place do you think?'

'*Chalo hato.*'

'What does that mean?'

'Stop messing about.'

'*Chalo* and *hato* - two new words.' Tommy sighed deeply, overacting. 'Parvin tell you about the roof, did she?'

'The roof?'

'A lot's happened.' Tommy was desperate to hold her, be alone with her. 'The Spinning roof.'

'*Jee haan*?'

'Destroyed, it was - caught fire.'

'Destroyed? Why didn't she say? Silly cousin. She's hopeless. Was anyone hurt?'

'Two welders, not that seriously in the end. Eight fire engines, and there's Mr Atherton inspecting the damage and looking like someone's just died.'

Sunehri said quietly, 'I have not met Mr Atherton Tommy, and I'm not surprised he was looking sad. What happened to the workers?'

'Went to hospital.'

'No, the other workers.'

'Oh, right. Well, they set up these enormous gas heaters

188

sending warm air down the alleyways between the machines so everyone could work through.'

Sunehri looked surprised. 'I see.'

Tommy tipped his head. 'There's always been a lot of hot air blowing round those spinners!'

She didn't take the joke. 'They don't complain?'

'About what?'

'Working outside with no roof. Are they working through the night, Tommy? Is there not a law against it, in this country?'

'Roof's mended now anyway.'

Sunehri had heard enough about the factory. The wind rattled the leaves and she re-tied her belt to keep the layers in place. 'Oh, that doesn't feel good. How cold do you find it? Not much I think, by the look of you.'

'It's real leather. Keeps the wind out better than a stupid cardigan any day.'

Sunehri locked Tommy's fingers in hers. There was no one around, well no one she recognised. 'What would Mrs O'Reilly say Tommy, if she saw us like this?'

'What's my mam got to do with it?'

'Well then, what if my maa and naani came walking down that path there, towards us?'

'Your banana came walking down that path there?'

'*Naheen* Tommy, my grandmother. What would she say?'

'I have no idea.' He sensed that if the two of them became serious... weren't they already serious? His mam sometimes commented on *them couples* as she called them, when they were in town. She could be tough, but she'd always acted fair when it came down to it. And wouldn't they both want what he

189

wanted? Not necessarily.

Sunehri moved closer and Tommy grabbed her round the waist. '*Muyay naheen patta*, Sunehri. I properly realised it when... look, can't we go somewhere?'

'Tommy, you have forgotten how to say it. You say it more like: *Mujhay... naheen patta*.'

'Who cares! I can't get everything right.' He broke away, dribbling a phantom ball. 'That match with Ribble Motors, they were better, and here comes their striker's pass but here's Jacko intercepting and YES, it's straight into the back of their net!'

Sunehri ran alongside. 'Good moves, Tommy. What are those trees called?'

'Chestnuts.'

'Tommy, you still have not answered my question.'

'I have, they're chestnut trees, conkers, for hardening in vinegar and threading with string and competing with. We can have a competition. I always win. Sweet chestnuts are the other kind you grill and eat, if you can get past the prickly cases.'

'I did not mean that question.'

Tommy kicked a stone through a hole in the perimeter fence. 'Well, what question?'

Sunehri was surprised that they'd come full circle. 'I'm not really sure.'

'Let's ride the Dodgems,' he said. 'A fourth go will feel completely different.'

She looked at her watch. 'What about the procession?'

'What about it? It'll take an hour to get to town once they've finished faffing about here. Come on, I've just got paid.'

Sunehri smiled. 'We need to find a place at the edge of the

pavement, otherwise we will see little, Jamelia says. Jamelia is just about old enough, she says, to remember what happened last Guild.' Sunehri whispered in Tommy's ear, 'Though I think Mrs Jones must be over fifty and she has lived here a long time.'

Tommy nodded. 'She's as old as my mam and dad and they're ancient. Always have been.'

'Parvin came round to see if I would go to the procession and I said *naheen*. So she must not see me.'

'With me, you mean?'

Sunehri didn't answer. Why did everything have to be so complicated?

Tommy played with his sideburns. 'So, what do you think Parvin and your maa and abbu - is that the name for someone's dad? You've used *abaa* before. Anyway, what would they think about it? Seeing us together?'

'It is abaa, not abbu when you are talking about *my* father. You have not even met him.' Sunehri's face looked pinched.

Tommy didn't notice the effect he was having. 'Well, I reckon he would absolutely love me. Try it, introduce us when he's next over here. See what happens.'

When Sunehri spoke again her voice was faint. 'If we want to walk with everyone else, Jamelia says they gather on Garstang Road. We are on the wrong side of the park.'

'Do you think I don't know which side of the park we're on?' Tommy didn't feel like doing what someone else wanted, especially Jamelia Jones.

By now they were standing outside the rim of the Dodgems.

Sunehri crossed the black rubberised floor. She knew it would turn lawless when the power in the wire-meshed ceiling shot

191

through rods attached to the cars. She had watched people on the Dodgems many times before.

'This one,' she said. 'I'm driving.'

40

Possession

They scrambled arm in arm away from the ride, but the bond they had begun to re-establish when enclosed in the squat car drifted into uncertainty and shyness as they stepped onto the muddy grass.

'Let's try this next.' Sunehri broke away and stood in front of a circle of grimy water where plastic ducks with loops in their heads floated round. The stallholder was pacing like a caged animal.

Within minutes Sunehri had caught a duck with her pole. The stallholder unhooked the bait and plonked the bird back in the water. 'Beginners' luck,' he grunted as he plucked a prize duck with a matching number from the central stem. He dropped it in Tommy's hand.

This seemed strange to Tommy. He recognised the man's face, from school maybe? There had been a Jim Wilcocks in the year above. This bloke looked far older, but he had the unmistakable features of a Wilcocks.

Sunehri manoeuvred the plastic beak to say in Tommy's face, 'Quack! We are quits. Is that what we are, quack-quack?'

'Yeah, suppose.' Not fully registering her words and aware of the stallholder's eyes on them he said, 'Let's get going.'

Sunehri brought out the little bag of coloured yarn as they walked towards town. '*Shukriya*, Tommy. It is very special.'

'Reet good, in't it. That's what my mam says all the time. Drives me mad.'

'Reet good,' Sunehri copied. She caught Tommy's hand, seeming oblivious now to who might see them. 'I have a present for you. I did not know you were coming so it's not here. I did not bring it.'

Tommy couldn't get the fairground bloke out of his mind. 'I didn't know you were coming either, did I.'

She quacked the duck in his face again, happy at the thought that he must have carried the silk winding everywhere with him. 'Tell me about this.'

'No, tell me what you were doing, out there,' he said. In their first seconds he'd looked for a ring. The fact that there wasn't one didn't say anything about her plans.

'You first. What have you been doing, Tommy?'

'Making a new shade for the Guild flags, for the background cloth. Me and Frank, we did it together.' He pointed to her hand. 'It's that shade. We've called it Glory Gold.'

Sunehri moved slightly away from him and Tommy was confused. She was remembering the time in their den when he had mimed a lamb holding a flagpole under its front leg and they had laughed and kissed and she had so much wanted to lie with him. Now, she said simply, 'Where are these new flags?'

'In town. If not there, somewhere else.'

'Really! Well, I want to see them.' Sunehri broke in to a run and they took short cuts towards the High Street using narrow alleys that had hardly changed since Victoria was on the throne.

'Your Mr Postlethwaite, Tommy, do you call him "Frank" to his face?'

Tommy slowed to catch his breath and Sunehri was grateful. He'd never been asked that before. The truth was, it went beyond names. He thought of Frank Postlethwaite as a second, or more like a third level, dad. Like a *general* dad if there was such a thing. He didn't know the name for it. *Uncle* maybe? 'What's the word in Urdu to describe a man who's like family but isn't related?' he asked her.

'Uncle.'

'In Urdu.'

'There are lots of words for uncle.' She smiled. 'Uncle in English is fine. Tell me some things about Frank your manager.'

It felt strange hearing her call Mr P by his first name. 'He's called Mr Postlethwaite - he *is* my boss. He's getting married.'

'Well, the manager in the Coning is very wise because I am getting my old job back.'

Tommy wanted so much to kiss her, but they were in broad daylight in the middle of town. If she was returning to work they could be alone together again! Then he remembered the den. Destroyed. He would have to tell her. They could find somewhere new. The main thing was that she had come back.

Khush, Sunehri was thinking. She liked the way he looked when he was properly happy. 'A new girl has started,' she said, 'in Tahira's place?'

'Yeah, Jenny she's called.' Tommy was thinking, *But how long will you stay?* He wanted so much to ask Sunehri about Pakistan. At the same time, he didn't want to ruin it now she was in the same part of the world again.

'I am looking forward to meeting Jenny and seeing Michelle and Maryana and the other girls. I am a bit worried too, Tommy, if I can remember those double...' She made the movement with her fingers.

'Doodly thingy knots? A cinch.'

'How would you know? You have never even made one.'

'A weaver's knot it's called. My mam taught me and her mam taught her and her...'

Sunehri laughed. '*Waghaira, waghaira.*'

'And once you've learned it you never forget, like riding a bike. Hey, it's your birthday before you start, *re-start* work.'

Sunehri looked at the clouds scudding across the sky.

'Have you heard about that street party?' Tommy said, trying to sound casual.

'I was just thinking,' she said.

'What's up? I suppose you couldn't exactly call it private, but we're both invited so there's no need to hide why we've both ended up there.' Tommy found another stone to turn into a football. 'If I decide to go.'

Sunehri chased him, sneaked a kick between his feet and dislodged the stone, keeping possession for a few yards until Tommy got it back and scored into a rotten tree.

'You have just crushed a hundred insects.'

'Sunehri, let's go somewhere, anywhere! We can do what we like. Can't we?'

'I went on a day trip.'

'Thought you preferred going away for a bit longer.'

She ignored the jibe. 'To Southport, on the bus.'

Tommy screwed up his face. 'Boring.'

'It wasn't. I liked it. What are you doing for your birthday?'

He found the question too hard to answer. 'Teach me some new words.'

She smiled. 'Now?'

'Yes.'

'What?'

'I don't know.'

'All right, concentrate. Here is a good one: *Mujhay Tommy O'Reilly say saab se ziyada piyaar hay.*'

Tommy scratched his chin, pretending not to know.

'You need a shave.'

'I need a shave,' he copied. 'Don't you think I've tried to find out what love is?'

She thought he looked gorgeous and *bohut piyara* and lovely.

Tommy tried it: '*Mujhay Sunehri Saleem say saab se... ziyada... piyaar hay.*'

She smiled. She had just heard Tommy say that he loved her the most. 'What will I tell my maa and Parvin I have been doing all day?'

They walked closely together.

Sunehri kept her hand on the braid inside her cardigan pocket. The prize duck was making the other pocket bulge. She had no idea where she would put it at home, only that it would have to be out of sight.

'I've decided something.' Tommy speeded up. 'I'll be middle-aged by the time the next Guild comes and you'll be...'

'Middle-aged,' she said.

'Oh yeah. I hadn't thought of that. That's quite funny actually. Come on, let's go and watch this procession.'

'What have you decided Tommy? Please tell me. It sounds important.'

'I'll tell you later.'

41

Waving the Flag

The crowds grew bigger the closer they came to the procession route. To Tommy this meant either more opportunities to hide or more chances to be caught.

'I've got a good story from 1952,' he said as they made the final ascent. 'Want to hear it?'

'1952? You have a good memory, Tommy!'

'Don't be daft. Listen. In Guild Week, my dad went skinny-dipping down by Horseshoe Bend with some mates from the foundry.'

'What is skinny-dipping?'

'Hold on.' Tommy paused in a doorway and Sunehri stepped under the arch with him. *A new place to mark on a brand new map?* 'So, the foundry boss's wife, she's out walking by the river with her dog, and the dog takes particular against my dad and it won't stop yapping. Dad's probably coughing by now. It's horrible in that foundry - the air's that claggy he's coughing up every morning even in the holidays. I'm glad I don't have to work there.'

'I am glad too, Tommy. What is skinny-dipping?'

'Dad was really worried he'd get a warning or something. But there was no mention of it, them being starkers standing on the riverbank in full display. The boss's wife must have kept the secret, and her dog.'

'I see,' Sunehri said, not completely seeing why it was funny.

They walked on, and after a few tries found a spot at the edge of the pavement with a good view of the marching bands blasting towards them down the road.

'My dad says it's the same bands that play in all the processions, for all the religions, Catholic and Protestant and the others in between.'

'What are the others in between?'

'Nonconformists. Think I'd have a lot in common with them.' Tommy felt happier than he'd ever been, but that bloke at the fairground bothered him, the way he'd ignored Sunehri.

She squeezed his hand. 'This is for everyone isn't it?'

'I don't know. It should be. Are you not having a good time?'

'I don't mean that, Tommy. It's just, there aren't many people who look like me.'

'Nobody I've met looks like you.'

'You're being soppy.'

'Sorry, I didn't mean it as a compliment - you took it the wrong way.' Tommy pointed to a tuba player and said over the noise, 'Look, not a finger-mark on that metal. Hey, if Aaron was offered a tuba, do you think he'd learn to play it, polish it every day? Or he could cash it in! I bet he'd cash it in.'

'I can't hear you, Tommy.'

The Protestants approached, solid leather straps slung from their necks holding cups where the wooden poles slotted in. Above them ornate, embroidered banners celebrated the Union with legends of 1690 and the Battle of the Boyne. As the shiny tassels flew this way and that with the force of the step, Sunehri thought how different the heavy brocade looked from the soft tassels she and her young cousins made from homespun wool.

The volume of the music dropped and Tommy took his chance to speak again. 'You know Sunehri, the three main churches used to come down this road at separate times carrying their separate banners.'

'Why?'

'To prevent clashes, sectarian clashes, and probably some other reasons but I don't know what they were. Once, the Protestants were running late and the Committee stopped the Town Hall clock for fourteen minutes to make sure they didn't come into contact with the Catholics.'

'Tommy, Jamelia was saying about the Catholic banner from the St Martyrs church. She said it might not come out today because it is quite windy.'

'Oh yeah, the King Kong triple size banner that needs four men to carry it and another four to take charge of the guiding ropes. No girls holding the ropes and doing a bit of dancing. Shame if we don't see it, I suppose.'

Sunehri touched his arm. 'I still can't see your flags.'

He shrugged, and pushed some change into a Rotary Club tin coming down the line. The rattling set a toddler off bawling, but when another brass band with a Drum Major came along hurling her silver-topped mace and catching it by a whisker, the crying stopped.

Tommy was fascinated by two children pincering clouds of candyfloss between thumb and forefinger and posting the sugary parcels onto their already pink tongues.

Sunehri pointed. 'There!' She pushed through the crowds and he followed.

They used up what money they had left to buy eight flags - for his mam and dad, Mrs Saleem, his grandma and Aunty Eileen, one for Parvin and one each for them.

'Hey, Sunehri, what about your abaa? They're light. You can take the flag off the stick and send it by post. It wouldn't cost that much. Why don't you give him Aunty Eileen's for now?'

At that moment Sunehri Saleem did not want to be the daughter of someone who...

Tommy hated watching her eyes turn glassy. 'Come on, don't cry. Your make-up'll run.'

'It is not funny.'

'I agree. That mascara's deadly.'

Sunehri knew he was trying to cheer her up but he was making things worse.

'Eh, Tommy!' It was Melville.

Tommy found a smile and Sunehri wiped her eyes as discreetly as she could.

'Seen a few familiar faces in town,' Melville said, 'no surprises there, but for some reason I didn't...' He moved aside. 'Meet my little sister Kate and her two kids.'

'Hello,' said Kate. 'This is Joseph and here's Barney.'

Sunehri bent down and shook hands with the children.

'So you've moved,' Tommy said to Kate. 'I'm pleased to meet you at last. Mel's told me, but I don't really know what's been going on, unless you see the local papers, the Belfast dailies I suppose, you can't...' He was getting flustered. What he really wanted to do was introduce Sunehri. It should be the most normal thing in the world. Then he realised his mistake. Melville must have seen Sunehri enough times in the canteen and round the factory. He might not know her name, but all he'd be interested in finding out was why they were here together.

Melville and his sister were looking directly at Sunehri.

Tommy shifted his weight from one foot to the other. He felt surrounded by people shouting, distracting him, waving his flag, messing up his thoughts.

Sunehri smiled. '*Salaam.*'

'That means hello in Urdu,' Tommy explained.

'I know, lad. Harry was teaching me a few words.'

'Uncle Harry,' Sunehri whispered.

'This is Mel from my laboratory and his family. Err, and this is Sunehri,' Tommy said.

'Great to meet you,' said Kate. 'Where'd you get those flags by the way? Cheerful, aren't they. Want one, boys?'

Melville put both hands up in submission. 'I didn't bribe her Tommy, I promise.'

'That woman still had a few left,' Sunehri said, pointing.

Kate went off with her boys. Tommy didn't feel like chatting. This wasn't going the way he wanted. *What did he want?* He wanted people to know. 'Mel, so it's really bad out there is it? My mam and dad went on holiday, but kept south.'

'Wise heads. It's pretty grim Tommy. Well, if it's facts you're after, this summer's claimed another hundred and four lives. 1972's turning out to be the worst year yet. Lots of innocents, some not so, but it's still individuals that used to be babies once, people's relatives, neighbours. The impact on the communities...'

'I am very sorry,' said Sunehri. 'I have read something about

The Troubles.'

Melville nodded. 'Four hundred and thirty-two killed as of yesterday's papers and we're only just arrived at September!'

The three of them stood awkwardly. Tommy and Sunehri were both thinking that whatever their current difficulties they were minor compared to what was going on across the water.

'That's why Kate's done the move really, for their safety.'

'What's that, big brother?' Kate handed a golden flag to Melville and kept one for herself. The children had their own. 'You don't *hold* a flag. Look at your nephews for a clue - you wave it!'

'Watch the cheek. Eh, I was just saying how you couldn't keep from coming to live at ours. My Sunday roasts was it that finally persuaded you?'

Kate laughed. 'Mel, the kids're running off again. Shall I go, and you come when you're ready?'

'Nah, it's fine. I'll be along.'

'Well, nice to meet you both,' said Kate. 'Going to the torchlight procession?'

Tommy looked at Sunehri then back at Kate. 'The carnival? The one at night?' He wasn't convinced Sunehri would want to spend her birthday watching men dressed in suspenders cavorting on floats, and scenes from horror films and musicals. Then again, maybe she'd enjoy it more than him.

Melville began to follow his family. 'You're both welcome to come to ours, after the carnival. By then we'll have done the unpacking, moved a bit of furniture round, blushed up, Tommy Red.' He smiled at Tommy. 'Got you there. It means *tidying* up. Anyways, it'd be nice to have some adult company. Kids're

204

tiring, though I suppose I'll get used to them.'

Tommy felt chuffed. Completely chuffed. *Invited to go to Mel's with Sunehri? Openly invited?*

Sunehri intervened. 'That is kind.'

'Yeah, thanks,' Tommy said. 'I appreciate that, given you've a lot on yourself.'

'No worries. And enjoy the rest of your day.'

'Bye, Mel,' said Tommy quietly, thinking, *I wish he hadn't mentioned "Tommy Red" because now I'll have to explain it.*

As he and Sunehri watched a cluster of smaller banners with Bible scenes bringing up the rear of the procession and parishioners peeling off to their church halls, he wondered what they would do next.

Sunehri grabbed his hand and they stole away towards the riverside and the old Tram Bridge where the football pitches got sodden in winter. They found a bench, and when they were quite alone, they kissed.

She pulled apart. 'It is only fair, Tommy. I need to tell you something very important. Straight away.'

42

Home / *Ghar*

Tommy's heart was racing.

What did she have to tell him?

It was about marriage, wasn't it! Betrothal. Promises made while she was away, maybe before she'd even gone.

Why did he have to be so happy one minute and the next plunged into... 'What is it, Sunehri?'

'It isn't that, not what I think is on your mind.'

'What's that?'

'I would like to smoke one of your cigarettes please.'

'What're you talking about Sunehri? You don't even smoke.'

'I want to smoke a cigarette.'

Tommy started laughing.

'Why are you laughing at me?'

'I'm not laughing at you, I'm... look Sunehri, I don't have any cigarettes.'

'What do you mean? You did not bring them?'

'No, I mean I don't smoke any more. I gave up.'

Sunehri looked at him for a few moments and frowned. When she spoke again it was so thinly that Tommy could barely hear her over the noise of the river. 'When we met on the park earlier,' she said, 'you asked why I had not warned you about me going away.'

'Yeah, what were you playing at?'

'Please Tommy, you are not letting me tell you.'

'Go on.'

'I was not even going to Mirpur. It was supposed to be Maa helping with Tahira's wedding. Then Abbu scraped enough together for my flight and, well, I think Uncle Harry and my Uncle Naseem helped too. Tommy, we did not manage to see each other that day. I tried the Jet Room corridor and the canteens, hoping to see you. And your show - it was awful!'

'The show was awful?'

'No, I mean, *tumhe phir naheen milna tthaa*, and I could not tell you where I was going. I wanted to be with you. I felt lost, that we might not be together. But it was one week only. That was what it was supposed to be. Once we were away it was longer and longer. I wanted so much to write to you.'

'But you didn't, did you.'

'Tommy, it might make difficulties, do you see? A letter from Pakistan coming through your letterbox.' She started to cry.

'What is it, Sunehri? It's more than you not telling me you were going. It's more than not writing. Isn't it!'

By now Sunehri was sobbing. 'I *will* be telling you! Here, your flag.'

'It's your flag,' he said, taking it anyway.

She looked at him directly. 'Tommy, the day before the wedding, Abbu was finishing a job on the Dam. It went wrong.'

'Went wrong?'

'It is hard enough as it is. Please let me speak.'

'Sorry. I mean it, Sunehri.'

'It was in the papers. It said, "Rabah Saleem, killed in an accident on the Mangla Dam, aged 51." This is all he was, and he is dead!'

'Oh, Sunehri...'

'So the wedding, it cannot go ahead when it is supposed to because of Abbu's burial, and then Tahira must still have her wedding because his family has come from the country and our family is there already and Maa is... What do you do when your husband, when the sadness comes and it will not go away? Poor Tahira, to have her wedding like that.'

'I'm glad you saw him, your dad, before it happened. You did see him didn't you?'

Sunehri nodded. 'The weekend before the wedding, yes. It was important. We were happy.' She brought out the golden-coloured yarn from her pocket.

Tommy squeezed her hand.

'I would like,' she began, 'I would have liked very much to send him this beautiful colour that describes my name. Perhaps I might tell him some of our story, Tommy O'Reilly. This flag, one for him too. I wish there was one for him too.'

'Sunehri, I do understand why you went away, and why you stayed away. But why so long?'

'We might not return at all. At first Maa says she will not leave his body, and so we will both stay in Mirpur with my grandparents. But Tommy, all the time I wished so much to come back to where you are. Even though Abbu died there.'

They hugged each other.

'What does that really mean though, Sunehri? How much do you want it? You called Mirpur home, before.'

'This is my home, whether it is with you or without you.'

'*Mujhay naheen patta*,' Tommy said, familiar words of doubt that took on an optimistic ring now that she was by his side. 'I was confused. You're right Sunehri, what you said about home. But you're wrong about not knowing what to do.'

She leant forward and placed her cheek against his. 'Am I? Why do you say that?'

'I don't know.'

They sat in silence for a long time.

'We can see a children's mime on the way up through Avenham if you like,' he said gently.

'What is this?'

'This teacher came into Cuff's and my mam was saying about it. Thirty schools are doing a mass enactment of the inside workings of a weaving machine.'

'That must be a lot of children.'

'Millions.' Tommy looked at his watch. 'I think it's already started. We don't need to go...'

'Look, Tommy!'

They saw a huge shape travelling across the sky, its enormous size making it appear low and slow-moving. As it approached they saw that it was a huge metal bird with a pointed beak.

Sunehri was about to say 'Concorde,' when the air was filled with a deep boom followed by ripples of sound that enclosed them in a bubble.

The sound gradually faded and they couldn't see the plane any longer.

Tommy flicked his hair. 'Twice the speed of sound, that's what it can do.'

'A Mach 2 *Parinda*?'

'Show-off! Well it was definitely not a teeny-tiny *chiriya*,' she said.

The arrival of the enormous plane had changed their mood. She touched his arm. 'Is it teatime, Tommy Red?'

'I hate Mel for that.'

'What does it mean, putting your name with *laal*?'

'I'll explain later.'

'Explain now.'

'That school display thing is about to finish,' he said.

She took his arm. 'So there is time to tell me how you got your nickname.'

As Sunehri and Tommy walked back, they welcomed the uncertainty about what would come next. They knew that tonight they would eat at different tables, but this was a lot better than the certainty of staying apart.

43

Viscose

My body is wrapped for a Sunday afternoon at home. Winter, reading, in front of the fire. I'm warm and comfortable except for a gale the draught excluder can't put a stop to.

The longer I am alone the more I feel trapped. Trapped in this room. Is that accurate? Enclosed by the words flowing from the page may be better.

I am by the river at Horseshoe Bend. I pause on the launch stone and dive in, naked. Water at the usual temperature, familiar sensation as my skin meets its wetness.

All other things are different. Take the flow rate, which is much slower than usual. I measure it from inside the water with a technical instrument that does not exist, that I remove from a pocket that does not exist.

The colour of the liquid - I haven't said - it changes from clear water to thick, flowing rust that catches the sun's gold, like rippling iron on a hot railway or as if seeing your life through a heat haze.

The rust-line grows solid as I observe my limbs moving inside it. Now swimming with difficulty, I'm dragged downstream to near the tip of the filament that twirls in acid like a ribbon in the air, its end flapping freely.

I do not want to come out at the end is the thought that takes me over as I swim from the Mixing Room through the ducts under Viscose Alley to the Caves.

I don't want to be here, not because of where I am but because of the faces I know I'll meet on the other side - Harry, Idzi, Naseem.

Harry, he's the one who really bothers me. I know that he wants me dead. If I don't climb out I'll become, well, see the headlines:

> **No longer human!**
> *Tiny male figure trapped in filament*
> *of viscose and woven into cloth...*

If I can get back to the river I can try and grab for that willow that's trailing its sapling arm out for me. I can use my strength to gain land. I can flop on the bank, my chest heaving.

Near to my face I see that broken branch. I have made it less solid than the yarn regenerated from cellulose by inventors in laboratories across the world. I mourn for the tree, a little, but it caused me to survive.

I find myself upright, both feet dripping with amber.

On the launch stone again, in the right position for a dive.

I don't want to dive.

That is the only thing I can be sure of.

44

We've Company

The world had come back to him. Or maybe he had come back to the world.

It took until midday before Tommy was foundering. What next? They hadn't even talked about what next! He had been left with the sense that there would be something, that was all. But what? Would *she* make the next move or was Sunehri waiting for *him*?

By twenty-five-past one he was unable to think straight. All he knew was that nothing had changed, not really, and he knew that nothing would. She lived round the corner and she might as well be in Pakistan for all he was doing about it.

'Going out,' he announced.

'Be back by four,' his mam said.

'Why?'

'Because.'

Instead of walking to Sunehri's road he went the other way to The Acregate.

He began with three pints of bitter and followed it with two whiskies. There wasn't much conversation going. Not the kind of conversation he was looking for. He walked to the nearest Off Licence, bought some cans and took them round to Jacko's.

Jacko was up for playing football, but when he saw Tommy he invited him in for a cup of instant.

'Sober you up, mate.'

'I don't want sobering up.'

'You do.'

'No I don't.'

Tommy slumped on the settee and opened one can of lager after the other.

'You eaten? Bet you haven't. You need to eat if you're drinking like that. Why're you drinking like that?'

When Tommy stood up he was swaying. 'I'll go home and eat something.'

'Have something here. I was going to cook anyway. Beans on toast.'

'In that case, I'm off.'

'You be all right, getting home?'

'Don't be soft. It's only round the corner.' *Round the corner.*

'That's the most sensible thing you've said since you got here. Get going then.'

It took Tommy a while to reach home, and longer to find the keyhole. Once inside he dragged some coats off the rack and stumbled over his dad's work boots.

'At last! Tommy.'

'Leave off with your meddling, Mam!' He made it to the kitchen and sat down.

'You're late.' These words, spoken close to Tommy's ear, sounded strange, like his mam was telling him off politely. 'We've company,' she said.

Tommy shouted through the wall, 'So that's the smell. A

visitor.' He faced his mam. 'Well you know where you can stuff your syrup flapjacks.' He began rapping on the adjoining wall and soon built up a strong rhythm.

Frank O'Reilly came and stood directly in front of his son. He looked the most uncomfortable Tommy had seen him. 'Quieten it down, Tom.'

'Hasn't your VISITOR got the point by now?'

'Don't rile yer mam.'

'I bet it's some girl with a face like a lizard. Conversational skills of a worm she'll have.' Tommy smiled. 'A bum as...'

'Son.'

Tommy groaned. 'Where's the aspirin?'

'Make him a brew,' Annie said to Frank before returning to the front room.

'Aspirins? Same place as always.' Frank's long frame reached for the medicine cupboard. He shook out two tablets and handed them over with a full glass of water. 'Drink the lot before thinking about coming in. Don't embarrass yerself. By the way, thee hairstyle's gone a bit skew-*quiff*.' Frank was hoping to raise a smile, but Tommy was too fuddled to notice.

He swallowed the tablets knowing that his mam and dad were sick of him being under their feet, and that was that. He'd be sick of him or her if he was her, or him, or something. The left side of his head began to pulse. It was time he moved out. He might kip down on Noel's settee for a bit until he'd saved enough for his own rent. Or Jacko might put him up. He'd ask Jacko first.

Tommy let his body fall to the chair-back. If he sat here long enough, years and years, whoever it was in the other room

215

might whittle themselves down to a skeleton, or a skellington, as his mam called it. The Scary Skellingtons of Skeffington Road. Tommy clamped his hand over his mouth to suppress a laugh and then belched. He found himself squinting at a face that filled the door-frame. 'You're not bony enough for a skellington, sorry Mam.'

Annie O'Reilly shook her head, and under her scrutiny Tommy dropped his gaze and felt bad for everything he'd done in his whole life that wasn't completely perfect. 'I'm not perfect,' he said.

She came over. 'Don't sit thur. Get to bed and sleep it off.'

Curiosity cleared Tommy's thoughts. 'Who's it this time?'

'Come and see if yer that bothered. But behave.'

Tommy followed her in.

The table had been extended and there were two visitors in the house.

One was called Mrs Ayesha Saleem.

The other was called Sunehri Saleem.

45

Not Enough for Oblivion

Tommy dropped a hand to the sideboard to steady himself. The room felt less familiar. Everyone but Sunehri was looking at him. The only person he was looking at was her. Sunehri was sitting in his front room.

Tommy ran his fingers through his hair and felt her fingertips stroking the soft skin of his earlobes and skittering all the way down his neck.

He stared past the guests to the once luxurious curtains, like something from the theatre, deep velvet bunches at each side, over-filling the space, cast-offs from his Aunty Lily who spent more money on expensive things than time with her family.

He dared a glance at Mrs Saleem. *Hello... salaam alekum. I don't know you, do I. No, that's right.*

His mam signalled for him to sit down.

'Sorry,' he said, feeling sick with beer. Keeping the belches in was making it worse. He saw the two of them side-by-side with the candle blown out and the warmth of their breaths closing off the world, desire in their lips, intent on something more than flesh and blood.

Sunehri looked straight at him.

What was she seeing? Eyes the colour of Mirpur Lake, a line

of freckles scattered like sesame seeds across his cheeks? *She said that, she always said that. And next she would be thinking about the rest of his skin hidden from view. Maybe not, maybe that was just him.*

He smiled. He should do something. He was behaving like a complete fool just standing there.

He noticed Sunehri check on her maa and his mam, who were talking, and then she pulled her tongue out at him.

Tommy's impulse was to grab her and kiss her and… but he couldn't get his thoughts straight. *It's what they both wanted, wasn't it?*

He hadn't drunk enough for either oblivion or clarity, just the right amount to understand the danger of failing. He registered bits and pieces of conversation about what Pakistan was like in the summer (usually dry) and what Preston was like in the summer (usually wet). Sunehri and her maa knew about both, whereas the O'Reillys had only fifty percent of the story.

'Sit down, will yer,' his mam said to him. But Tommy kept one leg pressed against the solid sideboard and listened to his mam launch into Gertie Godber and the tea party, then on to memories of previous Guilds. He noticed his dad looking concerned. Mrs Saleem had lived here on and off for enough years to know the details.

The moment his mam stopped talking, Mrs Saleem said, 'Mr and Mrs O'Reilly…'

'You can call me Annie.'

Mrs Saleem smiled. 'Thank you for the kind invitation.'

'Thank you,' Sunehri said, standing up and looking obviously at Tommy.

Frank helped Mrs Saleem and her daughter on with their light coats in his courteous way. 'Good yer could come, like.'

Because Tommy was concentrating on the embarrassment of his mam making a curtsey to Mrs Saleem, he missed what Sunehri said when she handed a small parcel to his dad.

Tommy watched as Ayesha Saleem took her daughter away from him all over again. *So what was he going to do about it?*

He collapsed into his dad's armchair.

That was probably the longest tea they'd had with anyone outside family, and he'd been absent for most of it.

He'd wanted this for so long, for her to come to his house.

'For you, Tom.'

Tommy grabbed the parcel from his dad and ripped it open. Inside was a tassel, knotted and wound in ochre and red and orange, like a ball of sunlight with woollen rays streaming outwards. There was no message.

He checked again. Definitely no message.

Tommy threw the tassel across the room and it landed in the clean fireplace. 'What're you both staring at?'

'She's beautiful, son,' his mam said, in that voice that had soothed his recurring bouts of fever as a child.

'Plenty of time,' his dad said, 'plenty. Then again, I haven't done owt about them racing tips fer tomorra.'

Tommy shifted awkwardly. He had to ask. If not now, never. 'What the hell was that all about? What've you two been up to behind my back? It's pathetic!'

Tommy's dad made for the door. 'Better get on.'

'All reet, Frank,' said his mam. 'If yer must.'

Frank took his cap from the hook. 'An hour at most.'

What was his dad talking about? It was a disaster. *There isn't plenty of time, there's no time at all!* Tommy looked at his - his dad's - watch. Just after six-thirty. One more failure.

'I'll mek us something proper: sausages, mash, peas.' Annie said to Frank's coat. She wasn't seeking approval. 'Me and Tommy can talk.'

The door closed.

Secrets. They'd gone behind his back while he was too busy dreaming and feeling sorry for himself.

When Tommy stood up he saw a folded piece of paper on the sideboard. It was the same size as all the other notes from her. He grabbed it and walked out, making sure he couldn't see any more of his mam's face than he needed to.

'Where're you off now, Tommy?'

'No idea.'

With his back to the house he shielded his eyes from the sun. *Mrs Saleem must have come here for a reason or she wouldn't have been sitting round their table, would she!*

He stood with his feet hanging over the edge of their step, reading over and over again the name that was scrawled on top of the note.

His name.

Inside, the message read:

We can go to our den.
Our birthdays soon! Maybe
we will see each other at
the street party first?

Remember what Melville
said about the torchlight
procession and... that *I love you.*
May tum say piyaar karti hoon.

S x

46

That Handkerchief

Tommy stayed where he was and re-read the message a dozen or more times.

Did that mean both their families were allowing it to happen? Him and Sunehri together?

It didn't make sense.

He closed his hand round the piece of paper and ran down the street.

Sunehri's aunties and uncles agreeing, his mam and dad agreeing? They must have.

But what did it have to do with any of them? He didn't want people arranging things for him. He wasn't a baby.

Maybe he was a baby.

Tommy turned the corner into Sunehri's street.

What next?

Since her abaa was dead, her uncles would have something to say about it. But Sunehri was eighteen on Saturday and she could do what she liked. *Couldn't she?*

Tommy approached her road.

In the next street, unseen, returning from the betting shop, was his dad. They reached the corner at exactly the same moment.

Tommy knocked his dad violently against the wall and there was the sound of a cheekbone hitting brick.

All he'd wanted was to get to Sunehri's house, talk to her, not let her go again, do whatever was needed. And now he'd gone and hurt his dad and he was stopped.

Tommy bent down to the figure lying crumpled on the pavement, blood streaming from a cut.

'Dad, hold on, I'll get my hanky.' It was Maureen Copton's handkerchief from the night of the rehearsal. He realised that he must have taken it out of the boiler suit, washed it and put it in his new work trousers to return it, then forgotten. The smell was still of her, talcum powder or similar which always made him think of bare skin. He waited for the smell of mashed potato. Nothing. The thought of Mr P and Maureen together, their wedding in October...

Tommy put the hankie to his dad's wound and held it there.

Frank covered his son's hand with his own larger hand and wiped his face. A thin streak of blood crusted the surface of his cheek as Tommy looked on.

'Dad, I'm really sorry.'

'I'll be reet, Tom.' His voice sounded weak. When Frank tried to get up, his legs collapsed from under him.

I need to go to her!

Tommy stuffed the bloodied hankie in his pocket and tried to steady his dad, to get him to a standing position, but his long frame gave way like a willow. 'Come on, we can get as far as home together, Dad.'

'I won,' Frank muttered, sounding far from victorious.

Was he concussed?

223

'But I lost it.'

Then it dawned on Tommy. His dad had been to the bookies, won money on the horses and then thrown it away on the next bet. It had happened so many times it wasn't worth mentioning. 'Who cares? We need to get you back. You might need the hospital or something.'

'I don't need th'ospital. Yer mam can sort it.' Frank's voice was gentle and kind as always, but insistent.

Tommy felt only love.

'What's happened here, friend?' It was Fons, standing in their way, wearing one of his aggressive purple shirts. *How many did he have?* Their dads worked in the same foundry.

Frank O'Reilly tottered. 'Sorry... How are yer, Alfonso?'

What did his dad have to apologise for? Tommy saw that Fons was holding out a £10 note.

'Dancing down the road it was.' Fons pointed. 'I caught it.'

'I bet you did,' Tommy said.

Tommy's dad looked at the money. 'When I fell... had two on 'em. Flew off, they did.'

'This must be yours then, Frank.'

Tommy hated hearing his rival address his dad like they were old mates.

Frank lowered his gaze and Fons gave him the money.

Tommy stepped in. 'Come on, Dad. Let's go.'

'Thanks, Alfonso,' said his dad.

But rather than leaving, Fons stepped in closer and addressed Tommy's dad directly. 'Need any help there, Frank?'

'Helped yourself already haven't you? I bet you pocketed the other tenner!'

224

Tommy felt a tug on his arm. 'Come on, son.'

Fons reddened, but he didn't move.

Tommy looked at him. 'Can't take a joke?'

Fons thought about it, then laughed over-loudly. 'The other one's long gone, mate, but if we see a bambino with a box of choc ices to himself we can ask a few questions, eh?'

Tommy looked at his dad, who smiled before wincing.

Frank O'Reilly was in a mess. 'Son, get off to wherever yer getting in such a hurry, I'll manage.' Frank looped his arm through Fons's.

Tommy felt like hitting his rival, then remembered Sunehri's message. *He had to get to her!* 'You be all right, Dad, going home with him?'

Frank O'Reilly put the money in Tommy's hand. 'It were fer yer birthday any road.'

Tommy was too flustered to say thank you. Instead, he watched his dad and Fons set off slowly towards home.

'See you in a bit,' came Frank O'Reilly's voice, too weak and too late for Tommy to hear it.

By now Tommy was registering the plain black number 2 on the front door of the first house in Sunehri's street.

At number 4 he heard his dad start with a coughing fit.

Should he go back?

Number 6, 8.

Still coughing.

His dad would be all right after he'd lain down for a bit. He'd sleep it off. He'd be all reet. Fons was all reet - wasn't he?

A few yards ahead of Tommy was her front step, mopped

and polished with red wax every Saturday morning, like his own, but unlike the rest of the neighbourhood who had dropped the custom a few years back. It made up for the landlord's unwillingness to repair the other parts of their rented house.

In one pocket Tommy fingered the note from Sunehri, in the other, the brown paper note that bore the Queen's head.

Number 10, 12. Tommy slowed his pace.

He breathed in a long breath.

He took his hands out of his pockets.

47

The World

Number 14, 16.

Harry and Naseem would definitely have some influence over their future.

Tommy stood in front of house Number 18.

He saw his mam's face, the greyness when minutes from now he'd come sloping back in, ready to tear more than his bedroom apart.

He banged on Number 18 with his fists. Old paint fell to the burnished step like snow on velvet curtains.

No one was coming!

They'd know it was him.

Sunehri's maa wasn't going to even answer.

Mrs Saleem opened the door. She looked concerned. Neither of them spoke. Tommy shifted from one foot to the other.

Where was Sunehri?

He looked down the street the way he'd come, and thought momentarily of his dad.

'Tommy?' said Mrs Saleem.

And there was Sunehri standing behind, her long *kaalaa* plait, her fine hands holding the threads of golden silk he had given to her, made for her.

Mrs Saleem turned to see Sunehri smile at him, in full view of the world.

Tommy took a step forward. 'Can I come in?

Ayesha Saleem moved aside and let Tommy in.

Epilogue

Holding your raggedy scarf made from an end of artificial silk and looking back to the seconds before the Mayor's ornate scissors had fully cut through the ribbon, it's only now, more than seventy years later, that I am beginning to understand.

The day the factory opened, the air at Atherton's was quiet for happy reasons. Of course I wasn't there, not right at the beginning, but I can see the council dignitaries lined up at the front, smiling at the thought of new investment coming in to the region, a chance to raise their profile too. I can see mill workers born in the town who'd lost their jobs in cotton, now eager to transfer what they could to the making of viscose. And so many new faces travelled across the world from India and the West Indies and Poland and Pakistan and dozens of countries, contracts of employment safely stored in their dressers at home, all stating better terms than they'd seen before: viscose-rayon, the new industry!

There's your dad, Sunehri, fresh and hopeful in his twenties, maybe standing on his toes for a better view of the Mayor, not knowing that he will leave the factory for even better terms on the Mangla Dam, not understanding how much you will miss him through your growing-up.

Though we weren't born yet, it doesn't take much to imagine the newspaper photographer that first day, ready to catch the moment when two ends of Glory Gold ribbon touched the earth - allow me that sentimentality, Sunehri - I've no idea what shade it was. It was the moment when the machines began to weave their stories.

Years later, there I am, just turned nineteen, on yet another visit, for the same reason as the one earlier in the day and the same reason from yesterday and the day before and every day for the three weeks since you started your job. I'm occupying the same table in the men's canteen, to the left of the opening to the Coning department.

And there you are, standing in Row 2 checking for broken filaments, frowning, concentrating. You turn to me and smile, not obviously. That's when it really began.

Let go, Tommy. You need to let go.

At least the children allowed me to come here today, to leave one dead place and come to another, though there's little or no satisfaction in that.

More and more I find myself having to ask permission. It's stifling and fussing and I don't like it. Laraib is the worst, stubborn, while Ghazala I can usually spin to my wishes. Imagine if I get to eighty - I can see our children not letting me leave the house!

No, I don't want anyone to come with me.

No, it's a short walk to the side gate. I can call you on the mobile if I need anything. Yes, I do remember how to use it.

A couple of hours will do. Don't come early or I won't be

there. I'll be waiting by the bus shelter. Yes, I promise.

Holding your hand at our bedside before your breath fell away, I whispered to your maa that I was sad about her childhood home in Mirpur, yours too, gone in that earthquake. Did you hear me? I told her the family would gather round. In the year since then they have. She asked to come with me today, your maa, come to your graveside, pull a few weeds, leave fresh flowers.

Not this time, I said, I'm sorry. You'll understand that I need to be on my own.

You might have heard me? I didn't want her to come along, to come along with me here, where we met.

Without you, Sunehri, no one's good company, that's the truth of it. I don't want anyone to see me here, father, son-in-law, worker as used to be, not sure of where I belong.

Not far from the side gate you are lying next to Mam and Dad, and coming to this dead factory today I find that you are gone from here too.

Except for this scarf. I might have gone a different way and never found your scarf. I suppose that in all these years of my staying away you've remained a part of it. Why doesn't that surprise me!

Here, I swam in the stream of amber liquid, a tiny human figure wrapped in a filament of artificial silk, always moving, making progress, belonging. Post Office Red and Tommy Red, the first and last shades we created at this factory, both of them *laal.* I haven't thought of that before, two reds saying two different things. *Look at us, we're just beginning!* And, *Can it really be ended? Already?*

231

After such a long while avoiding it I do have the feeling the old site's beginning to hum again. It isn't a steeping and pressing and Pfleiderising and churning and mixing and spinning sort of hum. There's not much of that. And the handful of small businesses occupying outhouses and bits of buildings that used to make up a whole factory, they don't appear to be adding as much to the world.

Let go. I need to let go.

As I sit here I can see that centre-spread in the newspaper, a headline saying "Street Teas are the Ticket!" or something about a ticket anyway. I remember the biggest photo. It was of our street party with the twenty-two-and-a-half tables pushed edge to edge. There's Gertie Godber squeezed between Julie Doherty and Betty O'Reilly, looking grumpy but tolerating it. Jamelia Jones, Mr Cuff and Falak Butt, wearing identical pinnies from Waverley Mill, are carrying battered old trays with squashed ant cakes and eyeballs made from buttermilk that over a lifetime you never persuaded me to enjoy. And Frank O'Reilly's lanky legs are stretched way under the highest end of the table at the top of the street and he's feeding runny lime jelly to little Debbie McGinty with a gentleness and grace that always forgave his shyness. For once, Annie O'Reilly is wearing a dress not hidden by a pinny. She's having a laugh with Ayesha Saleem and Mrs Cuff. And there's Tommy O'Reilly sitting next to Sunehri Saleem. Dicky N has a photo credit but there are no other name labels. There was no need - we knew the facts well enough. The children will remember some of it, but Sunehri there are so many things we've left unsaid.

Let go, Tommy.

So here I am, in some ways satisfied to find that our place to be alone remains alone. Then again, maybe that's not so good. I can't work out if it's bad or not. It doesn't feel bad. I wish I could ask what you thought, *mayri jaan*.

This morning when I opened my eyes I saw you again. I was on one of my visits, a flimsy excuse for abandoning dogsbody duties, running up the half-stairs and through the Spinning, down the corridors as long as Roman roads, coming to see you. Any reason was a good enough reason for seeing Sunehri Saleem. My dream dragged me away to the Pulp Store and I watched myself taking the stacked Collis somewhere, and when the lift doors clanged I was in our bedroom. I stared, awake, at my reflection, when all I desired was to see yours. I realised that I had no more control over this than my dream about seeing right through the house to its foundations and beyond.

Was it always you, pulling my perspective somewhere else, challenging me to see the world in new ways?

In a bit, when the children drive me home, I'll go straight up to our room and close the door. I'll sit on the bed so that I'm directly opposite that small patch of mirror where the silver paint isn't lost yet. I'll try to remember the beautiful colour of your skin, when I watched you in the mirror brushing your hair.

I know it's too late for that. You've left me for certain.

It really is too late.

Sitting on this pile of factory rubble wrapped in wild roses and convolvulus, before the felt-tip silhouettes arrive and I am gone, the tall oaks are still standing guard and the afternoon sun still looks my way. I admit to feeling afraid, yet for some reason...

233

'Look at you frowning, Tommy! It always makes your freckles squash together.'

'Sunehri!'

'Do not turn round, Tommy.'

'Why not? Of course I will, *mayri jaan*. I love you, Sunehri. Where are you?'

'Here I am Tommy. I am here.'

'Is it really you? Where are you, my love?'

'We are alone together, Tommy, like before.'

'Where are you? I can't see you! You made the shadows dance and brought me properly to life, but I can't see you!'

'*Maray jaan*, Tommy Red.'

'Sunehri, there you are - I can see you now. What a comfort it is not having to imagine your lips speaking those words to me. I knew those lips from a long time ago. I have you here, close by. Can I touch you? Are you so real that I can touch you and I'd be able to feel it?'

'Oh Tommy.'

'Sunehri, hold my hand.'

'Tommy.'

'But I'm weary about my life, what it will be like in...'

'You will be fine. *May tum say piyaar karti hoon* I love you.'

'Don't leave me again.'

'You will be all right, *maray jaan*.'

'Sunehri, don't go. Please.'

'It is cold, Tommy. Wrap my scarf around me.'

'Why leave now, when I love you more than ever?'

'I can't stay.'

'Me and you, Sunehri O'Reilly Saleem. That's all that's left at the edge of this world.'

'*Maaf kurna.* I'm sorry.'

'Don't go. Stay, for a while.'

'I must go, Tommy. *Mujhay jana hay.*'

'Let you go? How can I do that? Sunehri, you've just come back to me.'

'I'll never leave you, but I must go. Let me go.'

'I will follow you. For a short way at least.'

At the exact moment when two gossamer ends of ribbon touch the ground, and Atherton's, built for making artificial silk, is opening itself to the world like a flower, a world that wants it, you're walking away from me wrapped in a scarf of memories. Your grey-streaked plait is tapping your shoulder - that's me of course. Don't forget me. I know you're leaving this place for the last time. With the whole world toppled it hurts that Nicolas doesn't even stir as you pass by his gatehouse.

Look Sunehri! These hands over which I have less and less control, they're making the shape of *chiriyaan*, two birds flying away. If you turned back you would see them.

Alwidaah.

Alwidaah.

As free as a bird, that's what you always said. *Chiriya ki tarra azaad, tum kuch bhi kar saktay ho.* You could do anything you liked, you always said that.

You showed me the world, Sunehri.

My fear, *mayri jaan,* and perhaps it's not a terrible fear, more of an uncertainty, I'm frightened that these fingers are making the feathers of a single bird alone with its shadow. My shadow.

235

If I could, I would shorten the distance that's crept in, the distance between me and the life I used to live.

But you chose me and I'm more than glad. You, more than anyone, know that. Today, you've given me one more precious thing - I know that I need to tell the story.

Happy Birthday, Sunehri. I'm so happy we saw each other, today of all days.

I may not see you tomorrow.

Background notes

"The children will remember some of it, but there are so many things we've left unsaid..."

The region's industries have shaped its memories and left a lasting heritage, but there are many hidden stories. As the gap widens between the closing of the Northern textile factories and the present day, it's important to celebrate the unique experiences and perspectives of people who came to England to work in artificial silk (viscose) manufacture. Countries included Belgium, India, Lithuania, Pakistan, Poland, the Ukraine and the West Indies. Some Italian prisoners of war who were held on Moor Park in Preston settled and went on to work at Courtaulds Red Scar, a viscose factory in the North West of England. The fictional story *from Pakistan to Preston* reflects these and already resident communities.

Viscose Manufacture

Was it possible to make a type of silk that didn't require looking after and harvesting silkworms?

Dr Robert Hooke, the English physicist who discovered the law of elasticity, was fascinated by the way silkworms ate mulberry leaves and processed the cellulose into filaments that were excreted as silk thread.

In his book *Micrographia* (Small Drawings, London 1665), Hooke explored the possibility of imitating silkworms by making 'an artificial glutinous composition' and finding 'very quick ways of drawing it out into small wires for use'.

A century later, towns in the North and Midlands including

Congleton, Stockport, Derby and Macclesfield were still relying on silkworms to produce material that had the characteristics of silk. Macclesfield, in Cheshire, became the world's biggest producer of real silk.

In 1842 Louis Schwabe, a German-born silk weaver who had established a business in Manchester, presented a paper to British Association scientists. Schwabe had designed a machine that forced molten glass through the jet holes of a spinneret (which is like a large showerhead - this method features in the story). Threads made of glass were impractical, so he asked the scientists to help him find a more commercial solution; it wasn't easy to come by.

Patent after patent

It took until the year 1884 for Hilaire Bernigaud, the Count of Chardonnet, to take out a patent for the world's first artificial silk. He exhibited some samples at the Paris Exhibition in 1899 and received enough interest to build a factory in France, but his combination of cellulose and chemicals caught fire too easily.

Scientists and investors from many countries including France, Germany, Switzerland and the United States made patchy progress in the development of artificial silk. It may have remained an evil-smelling and explosive curiosity if not for the English lighting designers Charles Stearn and Fred Topham, who at the end of the 1880s were attempting to make filaments for electric lamps.

The fierceness of competition to develop artificial silk at this time is demonstrated by the frequency of patents. The patent taken out by Cross, Bevan and Beale in 1892 was for a commercially produced artificial silk or "viscose", a name which describes the smoothness or viscosity of the liquid before it is processed into lustrous yarn. The product was also called "rayon" from the French for ray, bright or beaming.

Courtaulds

Stearn and Topham's 1898 patent was for developing the continuous filament spinning process and the machinery needed to wash and collect the yarn. Courtaulds was the first to create commercial viscose by processing wood pulp, in Britain, in 1905.

By 1960 about two thirds of the world's man-made fibres were viscose, and refinements in the process continued to bring innovations. During the 1970s fine viscose fibres were woven into material for clothing, women's tights and flags (such as the 1972 Preston Guild flag in the story). Heavy fibres were used for carpets, and even heavier fibres for the carcass of car tyres - the inside lining of the rubber. Tyre cord accounted for a large part of Courtaulds' business when the site near Preston closed.

In the same way as 19th century chemists developed artificial silk, nylon eventually took over from viscose in the manufacture of tyre cord and textiles. During the 21st century viscose is still used widely, although biodegradable materials are increasingly in demand for surgical and sanitary products.

In 2012 two American chemists announced the development of artificial threads that mirrored the strength of spiders' filaments, which are stronger than the filaments made by silkworms.

Textiles building on textiles

In the story *from Pakistan to Preston* Mr Atherton's ancestor set up silkworm spinning in Essex, and the family's manufacturing expertise was built on to produce artificial silk. Similarly, the real Courtaulds family business had grown on the popularity of Victorian black silk for mourning dress before the advent of viscose, meaning that an investment in an alternative to silkworms would improve the pace and economy of production.

A textile town historically producing cotton was one of the British sites chosen by Courtaulds to construct a viscose plant. The Red Scar works north of Preston in Lancashire, North West England, was constructed over a large underground lake. Water is essential for making artificial silk, and this was pumped up from five out of seven bore wells. The water was too hard, so first it went to a softening plant. Laboratory workers like Tommy O'Reilly in the story needed to test the softness of the treated water before it was used in the boilers, for cake-washing and other processes.

As well as water, the factory required good transport facilities. Like the fictional Atherton's factory, Courtaulds Red Scar works had a branch line built from the main railway station - a spur from Preston to Longridge - that carried raw materials such as wood pulp from Scandinavia. An already good road network was improved when the first motorway-standard road in the United Kingdom, the Preston bypass, was completed in 1958.

And the factory needed labour. Cotton was the main employer in textile manufacturing in the North of England before artificial silk, and some cotton techniques were adapted.

Local entrepreneur Richard Arkwright's method for dividing labour, used in his horse-driven cotton spinning mill in Preston, strongly influenced the design of modern factories. The authors of this fictional account have based Mr Atherton on the real Mr Richard Arkwright, who demonstrated early creative and business flair in the dyeing and manufacturing of wigs that used waterproof dye. The Duracol pigments that transformed non-pigmented, off-white, spun viscose yarn into a myriad of shades in the 20th century were more resilient than dyes; in fact so resilient that they have not faded half a century later.

The terraced houses in Preston where Tommy O'Reilly and Sunehri Saleem live in the story were built for cotton weavers. As British textiles innovated, people adapted their skills (such as tying weavers' knots), which enabled some of them to work with artificial silk.

The Guild

When did the Guild celebrations begin? Why do they continue?

In 1179 King Henry II granted Preston the right to have a Guild Merchant. The Guild was an organisation of traders, craftsmen and merchants that controlled trade in this Lancashire town.

Every 20 years the Guild met to update its records, admit new members, and deal with people falsely claiming the right to trade. The gatherings were a good excuse to hold street processions. After the Guild lost its power in 1790, the Guild Merchant survived because the celebrations had grown into prestigious social occasions.

Preston Guild is the only one of its kind flourishing today, and it still happens every 20 years. The 1942 Guild was delayed by 10 years because of the Second World War, so making the recent Guilds 1952, 1972, 1992 and 2012. Unless something interrupts it, the next Guild will be in 2032.

Procession banners were usually made many years previously by the craft guilds, local industries, unions, churches and other community groups. The Guild tradition was for hundreds of Union Flags (Union Jacks) to decorate Preston's terraced streets, the Town Hall and other municipal buildings. In the story, the Mayor has the idea of commissioning Atherton's factory to produce a bright new shade for the background of the 1972 Guild flag.

For processions prior to 1972, the three main church groups were given separate slots with a sufficient gap to avoid sectarian-motivated trouble. Other religious groups parading with banners were the Methodists and Free Churches, and the Gujurat Hindu Society took part for the first time in 1972.

The Carnival or Torchlight Procession was on the last night of the Guild, a Saturday. There was no parade princess, unlike other North West street processions such as May Day and Whit Sunday. Atherton's day workers, including Tommy and Sunehri, were off for the whole of Guild week, which in 1972 ran from Monday to Saturday. Atherton's never closed, just like the real Courtaulds factory... except when over 2,600 workers were made redundant in 1980.

Language and dialects

Why are different forms of speech used in this story?

Roman Urdu is woven through the story. It is a phonetic way of presenting the spoken sounds of traditional Urdu Script. The phonetic spellings make it easier for non-Urdu speakers to experience its cadences and meanings.

Tommy O'Reilly feels an allegiance to Walter Greenwood's book *Love on the Dole* (1933) set in Salford in the North West of England. The broad Lancashire dialect of some of that book's characters resonates with the story *from Pakistan to Preston*.

Newly-written lyrics in the style of weavers' songs from the Victorian cotton mills capture rhythm, humour and social history in the Atherton Drama Society scenes in this new book.

About the Authors

Alison and Terry Boyle is a daughter and father writing team known as A.T. Boyle.

For 33 years from the age of seventeen until the factory closed in September 1980, my father worked in the laboratory of Courtaulds Red Scar in Lancashire, North West England. Many people met at the factory and got married. My mother and father were in the same lab for seven years before getting married. Their mothers were weavers in the same cotton mill in Preston for a time. Annie Boyle started work at 13 and remained in the same mill for 40 years.

Jean and Terry were members of the factory's drama club and Terry has directed and performed in regional venues including Southport's Little Theatre (playing the King in *The King and I)* and The Charter Theatre inside the Guild Hall. Preston's Guild Hall was built to replace the Public Hall, but its opening was delayed until the year following the 1972 Guild because of a builders' strike.

Terry was also the goalie in Courtaulds' football team. Both of my parents have provided advice on this fictional story based in fact.

As a published author and formerly an editor-publisher, for this book I went back to chemistry class and learnt a smidgeon of the many technicalities of viscose manufacturing, hardly written about before, as well as some Urdu.

Most of the narrative is set in 1972. For Preston Guild that year I took part in an outdoor mime with hundreds of local schoolchildren on Avenham Park, by the River Ribble. Pupils from my school and rival schools (fierce opponents in the Skittleball League) enacted the workings of a factory with its cogs and shuttles, chutes and other traditional cotton processes. A fly-over by Concorde stopped the human machinery below for several minutes, which is longer than would be allowed in a real viscose/rayon/artificial silk factory.

In the Sample Shade Books my father saved from destruction when Courtaulds Red Scar works closed, two out of the hundreds of colours created stand out for me: *Glory Gold* and *Tommy Red*.

Alison Boyle
Manchester, August 2012